Sifting the Ashes

a poetry collection

MICHAEL BAILEY AND MARGE SIMON

Let the world know:
#IGotMyCLPBook!

Crystal Lake Publishing
www.CrystalLakePub.com

WELCOME
TO ANOTHER

CRYSTAL LAKE PUBLISHING
CREATION

Join today at www.crystallakepub.com & www.patreon.com/CLP

Table of Contents

Blink

When you can't see them anymore,
    their outlines permanently flashed:
        against dirt, once grass
        against asphalt, and brick
        against will
    washed clean by endless tears
    they are never gone
    in death they still run:
        into the earth
        down drains
        from thoughts

Blink not to forget
    but to cover individually
    with pleasant-past
        / blink

When you close your eyes
    their lives inverted silhouettes:
        hidden in memory
        hidden from the children
        hidden inside
    washed away by a sleeve

they are gone
in reality you still drive:
        away from the flames
        down fiery lanes
        into smoke

Blink not to remember
        but to let go
        of the loss
                / blink

When you pick your random non-random moment
        their images temporarily erased:
                replaced by sandy beaches
                replaced with smiles
                replaced recursively
        from the mind over years
        they are forever
        alive and never still:
                but linger
                as reminders
                of compassion

Blink not for closure
        but to overlay
        one atop the other
                / blink

Prelude

You call me Mother,
but this isn't about you.

I make your home,
give you breath,
spider webs
and sap of trees
to mend your ails,
share the warmth of my sun,
life with my waters,

harvests
challenges
pain
wisdom

a place to live,
a place to rest.

You make a great deal of noise
as you rend and rape my body

Whatever now,
it's all on you;
my sisters
couldn't care less.

Forecast

100% chance of snow is expected at all elevations now through [time / date], starting at high elevations and progressing to sea-level overnight. 12-24" of coverage in rural communities, with light cover in surrounding areas and dustings elsewhere. Be cautious of falling trees, limbs, and other debris. Report arcing / sparking powerlines by calling 911.

This storm watch is in effect for the following counties: [all].

Now through the end of the week, high consistent winds are expected between 30-70 mph, with gusts in the high-40s to low-hundreds over the next 12-[TBD] hours, with insignificant reduction in wind speeds beginning [time / date]. Those living in impacted areas are advised to find alternate shelter.

A [fire]tornado watch has been issued by the National Weather Service and is in effect until [time / date]. When driving, avoid roadways, and make room for first- and second-responder vehicles, including police, sheriff, fire, ambulance, as well as gas and electric service vehicles.

Temperatures will remain in the 90s through the end of the week, with lows in the mid-60s. Heatwaves are expected all hours, ranging between high-hundreds and low twenty-six-hundreds.

An advisory is in effect to avoid high-heat areas.

Those living in mountainous regions, as well as those in highly-populated rural communities, are asked to stay outdoors for the foreseeable future, or to seek shelter at one of the following locations: [n/a].

This storm watch is in effect now through [TBD].

No other warnings will be issued.

Mon Autumn

Little pieces from me fall,
Jagged-jigsaw bits of memory
I try pounding them back in place,
But they no longer fit.
Their necks just bend

And so they fall / no longer fit

Little pieces from me fall,
Wadded-sticky bits of mind.
I try gluing them back together,
But they no longer stick
They just fall apart

And so they fall / no longer stick

Little pieces from me fall,
Fast-forgotten bits of past.
I try, I try, I try to remember,
But they no longer stay.
They just go away.

And so they fall / no longer stay

Little pieces,
These little pieces from me,
These things,
They fall.
I try,
These things,
But,
Like weathered leaves,
They crumble at my feet.
I step on my mind,
A labyrinth mind,
My mind,
All but ash.
Within my fingertips
Lies
My past.
I try,
These things,
Forcing them back inside,
But they no longer live.
They just get smashed.

And so they fall / no longer live.

Cold Tomorrows

The boy is worried. His little sister won't stop crying, and both of them are very hungry. His father left last week, dressed in many layers to ward off the cold. He said he was going to fix the generator but he didn't come back. Momma has gone to sleep and he can't wake her up. The cell phone is dead, no electricity, so he can't call the pastor or the school or the police. When he went outside, the winds were so great he barely made it back to the house. He looks at the supplies left. An Oreo cookie and a can of diet cola. Vaguely he remembers Pastor John's story about Jesus and the Last Supper. He makes his sister wait until he says grace. He gives her the last cookie.

Angel Wings of Death

Turning the handle
A mad wind takes hold
Pulling her outside
All three hinges shot . . .

There, a crackle
Takes her very breath
Amid a melee
Silent screaming mouths . . .

She joins the chaos
Steps on broken glass
No, she realizes
Black tumbling bay leaves . . .

They cover the ground
And spiral freefall
Casualties of war
Angel wings of death . . .

Sifting the Ashes

She holds out her hand
Catches one mid-air
An ugly snowflake
A chrysalis shell . . .

Crumbled by fingers
Still warm to the touch
What to make of it
All these dying trees . . .

Death-rain from above
Draws her attention
She looks to the sky
Eyes of hot embers . . .

Hero

White hot embers
barraging her trailer,
a fallen tree blocking her driveway,
Darlene can't budge it.

A light appears
on the empty street,
the squeak of chain,
a boy turns up on his bike—
brand new Schwinn
he got for his 12th birthday
two weeks ago on a Sunday,
but Darlene doesn't know that part.

He stops to help her (a woman
who his family calls trailer trash),
the boy doesn't judge;
even together, they can't move it.

Kid disappears down the road,
returns with a fireman in an SUV.
He wouldn't get in with her,
wouldn't leave his new bike,

so they left him racing the flames,
saying he'd spread the word.
She wonders if he made it out.

Two years later a bike wheel is found
in a mound of ash, frame melted,
tire missing, just past where
Mrs. Armstead's cottage used to be.

Nobody told Mrs. A. about the building renewal.
Being dead, she wasn't around to be notified.
Nobody knows what happened to the kid on the bike.

Orange Borealis

Mountain peaks stab the night in silhouette
A childlike rendition of a dinosaur's back:
Spreadicus bideathasaurus
Watercolor strokes, ever-morphing
       / an artist waving his brush
       / a mad-musician orchestrating

God, the painter
God, the conductor

Magic: there's a seemingly endless supply
Orange-yellow-red spreads
Bleeds through cloud bandages
Pulses muffled-raucous thunder from afar
       / propane explosion bass
       / bursting water heater tympani
       / vehicle bomb crescendo

The canvas spans the night
The band of orange borealis stretches miles
Approaching at the speed of sound

Next come woodwinds squealing through split reeds
Next come out-of-tune horns, calling as Sirens
Next come blending palettes of autumn alight
Next come wider brushes
      / a blind painter
      / a deaf conductor

God, of new-life's portrait
God, of the orange borealis band

Sorry

They'd argued that morning, Something about organic
bananas because they weren't the right kind,
according to his bride, swollen with their first child.
He watches the early morning news; she makes a racket
in the kitchen, banging pots and slamming cabinet doors.

A report about a rash of fires, but hey,
the newsman is so cheerful, can't be that bad,
he thinks, until he goes outside and checks,
to find the air is thick with smoke, a holocaust
of flames sky high, a mile off, maybe closer,
winds pushing the inferno straight their way.

They load up, searching roadways out, and finding none.
She moans, he hears her saying *it's started, Al, it's
started hard,*
sees her eyes so wide, face pale, perspiring, knows the next
words will be *my water's broke* and goddamn, he's right.
Fireman to hospital: "She's seized, now comatose . . ."

When an ambulance arrives, he follows close behind.
Inside, collapses on a clinic bench, surrounded by
a frenzy—nurses running, loaded gurneys, children's
    cries,
everything is "stet!" as sounds and conversations blur,
    until
"Sir, your son is fine, but though we tried our best,
    she's gone—
eclampsia. Could've been brought on by stress."

He mumbles something, garbled nonsense words,
breaks down sobbing, saying *sorry* to her many times,
    but
what he doesn't want to think about won't go away—
not one alert, and not another soul to say they're sorry.

Loosed Earth

A burning world
prays yearning for rain
during a pained draught
no doubt which comes
too late for some
to extinguish last hotspots
brought upon past soft plots
sending a simmering ground
glimmering with ash-mud
to slip-slide the sides
in scare-rides
not meant for women
nor men or children
caught mixed in the crud
in fraught games of chance
to play in avalanches of unstable
rubble unable to cling to root
and soot attempting to
hold a cold and crumbling
foundation together
and will this never end
or go on forever
as the terrible

treble-tremble sings
a sad ensemble
of oversaturated help
to sated gods
devoid of love
bringing new horrors
for hours or forever
as those coerced
to flee are freed
then forced to plea
on frayed knees
praying for heat
in dry pouts
as they cry out
for fires to mask the floods . . .

The Firegod Cometh

Embers arrive on windstream currents,
to ravage where they fall, changing
    lives forevermore with
    their horrid howling wisps and . . .
lands from green to blackened ash,
like Sherman's Union armies left the South
    we moved ourselves from the city limits
    to get away from overpopulation
    not long ago . . .
eight hundred years ago, so Vulcan's
soldiers march across Sonoma county.

Robert J. surveys his property,
    horses in the field, spooked,
    chickens cooped and caught . . .
suddenly alive with flaming lights,
bright mouths land to gorge upon his trees,
    wings and limbs afire . . .
his wife's garden, spreading closer
    now it grows, long given up
    more than a month ago,
    once providing food . . .
to their home of brick and Dougfir pine.

He'd insisted they'd be safe, so far
from the inferno to the northeast,
>   *so close, an entire mountain crawling*
>   *in the distance, the night aglow . . .*
but the fickle offshore winds change course,
a sideways rain of red-hot flakes, driven
>   *deep like the tips of cigarettes*
>   *buried into the skin, like mad father . . .*
fifty miles an hour slaps against the house,
>   *you will tell no one, boy!*
already it is past the time to flee.

He gets his ailing wife into their car,
>   *right behind you,*
>   *I promise . . .*
takes off down the road, but a fallen tree deters
their way, and Vulcan's minions are upon them.
There's but one thing left to do—he leaves
>   *fluttering hot onto the roof,*
>   *the fence line crumbling, freeing . . .*
his dear Marie, starts for help amid the flames,
but he is old, and help is fifteen miles away.

A Recursive Cleanse

Don't think this is the first time something like this has happened. No, not by a long shot. Nor will it be the last. Not a bad thing, either, this recursive purge. You'd think the most "intelligent" of creatures would learn the first time around, or the second, or third; that they'd simply use their feet to get out of the way. Alas, the lesser beings, those "not-so-intelligent," they have learned the routine by now. But humankind, no . . . The earth takes its hot bath, regularly, an easily-recognizable pattern, cleansing itself of its parasites, nature destroying the unnatural . . .

Diggin' Ghosts

In eighteen forty-eight a diggin's was settled
       nuggets the size of fists
       plucked from dyin' creek-beds
       panned out seasonal streams
       yeller collected dust

For in this placer-town some men was hanged
       not once, not twice, thrice

In eighteen fifty-love their gilted restless ghosts
       haunted the mines by night
       drunk on the chilly air
       swam splashless 'long long-toms
       nightmare'd the lone sleepless

And in this unestablished place of sin
       Miwok and Maidu wept

In eighteen fifty-two a fourth was strung up high
       same evil oak tree branch
       damn harbinger of death
       both feet all a-dangle
       afore off'rin' to jump

And in this establishment past recurred
    'cause Lynch's law was just

In eighteen fifty-four men gave name to a town
    one perhaps more pleasant
    Placerville was agreed
    a unanimous vote
    for fear chased away guests

And in this hang-town 'nother two years passed
    'til the first three returned

In eighteen fifty-six the whole town was burned
    not once, not twice, thrice
    each seemed to take its turn
    revenge served afire
    the fourth waitin' to spoil

For in this ol' dry diggin's there are hells
    one for each life 'was took

The Hanging Time

This isn't about what I did,
or what I said in court.
They all said I was guilty.
I killed someone,
it don't matter why,
'cept I'm part Miwok.

Cast shadows from
the bars on my window
stripes on my mattress,
no sheets, *"in case the breed*
tries to escape—"
that was a laugh.

The worst part was the wait,
with preachers
and crying women,
all that talk about Jesus.

Then the walk;
I stumbled
on the fourth step.
Nine more to go,

head bowed
watching my feet
proceed

to that hooded
white man on the platform—
I guess it was a man,
ashamed to show his face.

Fingers knot the blindfold,
drape the noose.
The darkness final,
a clean smell,
Sure can't be *their* hell.

Past the Past

life
hangs on
by a string,
so delicate,
a never-ending cyclical nightmare;
when will humankind learn how to listen
to sense, logic?
not ever,
until
death.

past
creates
illusions,
in retrospect,
premonitions of uncertain futures;
history repeats every so often,
all unprepared,
shocked by the
present,
now.

Sparking

At Tesla's funeral

His mourners' stream by
in a burning blue wail

Edison and Marconi
dispatch wireless electricity
with proprietary meanness

During the memorial service
someone in the back row
whispers fire

Transformers, blow,
power lines down
released into the wilds,
Tesla's crazed snakes
strike again and again

Arcing

It's safe, you're told, *not to worry*
about the soft *thump-thump* under tire,
no electrocution,
rubber wheels—
thump-thump, two axles.

Could be arms, legs
you tell yourself, *or a child,*
and what's not to say they're not
with visibility far as the windshield,
wipers smearing gray?

With a gust the wind shifts,
clearing your view of
(Armageddon, end of the world)
the driveway as dangling snakes
snit-snit strike against metal.

One slams against the hood,
it's okay, you're told, *okay . . .*
arcing from its mouth
and *don't panic!*
as it carves with a metallic hiss.

Michael Bailey and Marge Simon

Thump-thump go the tires, *thump-thump*
once again, a jounce
(not a dog, nor a cat),
perhaps a fallen limb, *from a tree,*
pulling down the lines.

Pacific Gassed & Electrified

Prelude, in F#

Board meeting on the exec floor.
One little, two little, three little CEO's,
kings of a vast domain exclusively
theirs and their stockholders.
Abernathy discreetly picks a scab,
Grenville pops a breath mint,
Smithson yawns.

Discussion of funds, expansion,
approval of this or that project,
no mention of the real problem,
the one that will bring them to their knees
before they will admit it exists.

On the 4th floor is Service Engineering.
Department head Bob H is a 3-pack a day smoker,
a tick begins when he smiles or tries to smile,
he's losing his hair and has sleep issues.

A prescription bottle of OxyContin and
a bottle of Absolut in the bottom desk drawer,
Bobby's secret little helpers.

Warnings, team reports and actions needed,
Bob removes such undesirable material as
instructed
before the folder goes upstairs to the Big Guys
who will assure the payments to shareholders,
and nothing to maintain the lines.

Alternate prelude, in F^U

Family meeting in the kitchen.
One little, two little, three tired sleepwalkers,
waking dreamy-distant minds
panicking over pounding fists.
Mom secretly whispers a prayer,
Elise fills an ice chest,
Sammy rubs his eyes.

Discussion to run, evacuate,
rejection of this or that necessity,
no word back from their god,
the one who will bring them to the streets,
and empty all their savings.

On the 1st floor is the Living Room.
Dad looking for his keys amid the smoke,
a cough when he breathes or tries to breathe,
he's losing his air and has anxiety.
An empty bottle of Citalopram and

a handle of Jameson on the topmost shelf,
Daddy's not-so-secret partners.

Warning, nobody thought to send one,
too late for the pets frightened upstairs.
Dad screams to go on without him,
rushes up two steps a time toward cries,
finds his daughter's silent cat,
the phone line dead.

Interlude, in F#

One and two and three little CEO's,
emergency meeting, impact of the fires
drags on for hours, a sushi lunch is ordered in.
Abernathy frowns, hates Japanese.
Grenville cleans his plate.
Smithson stands looking out the window.
Down on the 4th floor, Bob H paces,
seriously considering suicide.

Alternate Interlude, in F^U

One and two and three tired sifters,
a not-so-urgent gathering, prodding the ash
takes most the day, paper coffee cups emptied.
Lee grimaces, finding a femur.
Everson raises a skull.
Matheson kneels looking over the ruin.
Traversing foundation, they collectively sigh,
somberly reflecting homicide.

Postlude in F#

Board meeting on the exec floor.
One little, two little, three little CEO's,
one on the chopping block,
off with his liability head.
Abernathy tactfully feigns awareness,
Grenville points a fat finger,
Smithson squirms.

Discussion of blame, diversion,
an effort shown of this or that interest,
distraction from the elephant,
a solution that will bring them to bankruptcy
after already far too late.

On the 3rd floor is Personal Relations.
Specialist lead Jill M is a 3-glass a day drinker,
a tear glides down her right cheek at will,
she's curled her hair and has stage presence.
A loaded question about preventatives,
the reporter riling fellow journalists,
Jill's everyday trial.

Solutions, overtime and correction is needed,
Jill averts such accusations as instructed
before the guillotine beheads the next
who will discover shredded paper-trail bonuses,
and refuse to claim ignorance.

Alternate Postlude, in F^U

Family meeting in what was the kitchen.
One little, two little, three tired sleepwalkers.
Elise clutches her diary—the one with the lock,
so her brother will never know her secrets,
but the key is a lump of melted brass.
Sammy's eyes won't focus,
rubble and ashes, pipes sticking up
where their sink was, the bathrooms too.
This isn't real, isn't our house. It didn't happen.
He stiffens when his mother hugs him.

Dad silently pokes at the debris with a stick,
as if he could resurrect something familiar here.
Elise tries to reach him, takes his hand,
tries to squeeze some feeling back.

They're staying with friends, once strangers.
Mom sleeps with her purse beside the bed,
checks her cell is charged before she rests,
just in case, she tells herself, just in case.

The cat Dad had to abandon is found alive,
but now it won't go outside, howls for no reason.
If families don't want to talk about it, don't ask.
For them, it's never going to be over.

Dispatch

911, what's your emergency—Hello? Hello? Sir, can you speak up? Our connection's bad, you're breaking up and I can't—

Fire Medical Dispatch, this is—Yes, I can take the call. Click. Ma'am, I can't hear you. Did you say a fire? What kind of fire? Is this a structure fire? You're going to have to calm down—I can't—Can you confirm this is a structure fire?

911, what's your emergency—What do you mean the entire mountain? Sir, can you see flames? If you can see flames I suggest—So you can't see flames. You should be fine. Yes, I understand. The smoke, yes, it can travel miles. What's your address? Okay, sir, sir? Three is a fire reported already. That fire's well north of you. You should be fine.

911, what's your emergency—No, there are no evacuations at this time in your area. Yes, we are well aware—Dial tone . . .

Fire Medical Dispatch, this is—No, we just can't take any more calls, I'm sorry. We don't have the resources—Yes, I understand, transfer. Click. Hello, this is—What's your emergency?

Fire Medical Dispatch, this is—Hello? Hello? What's going on tonight. There's no one on the line. This is crazy. Hello? Beep, beep, beep, beep, beep . . .

911, what's your emergency—Yes, there are brushfires tonight, yes, we are aware. There's a fire in—Yes, that one's in—Ma'am, can you see flames? If you can— What do you mean trapped? Okay, someone's on the way. Dial tone . . .

Fire Medical Dispatch, this is—Yes, I understand the situation, but we just can't handle any more calls! We've already—

911, what's your emergency—

Hello? Hello? Are you there?

Sleep, Child

Go back to sleep, child. 9-1-1 says we're fine. The woman who answered sounded frantic, maybe inundated with other calls. It's so very far from here, miles and miles, she said, so not to worry.

Here, I'll tuck you in, kiss you good-night, the blanket snug, see. Now try to get some rest. Your window is closed to keep out the smoke. That crackling? Leaves, blown in from afar.

Don't mind the sirens, no, they're headed the next town over to help. Listen to their fading. Means they're headed out. That howling, not wolves, just wind pushing against the panes.

I'll close your curtains so the glow won't bother you, child, now close your eyes. So very far back in the mountains, don't worry. Seven miles, the woman said. A long ways from here.

No, I'm not sure who that might be at the door. I'll check, you sleep. Probably a neighbor, maybe anxious the power's out. You can keep your candle lit if it brings you comfort.

Dream happy dreams, child . . .

A House with Many Openings

I craved a house with many openings,
overflowing with your books & my paintings,
with room for children, & we were blessed—
the last was Jimmy, just turned three.

We watched our neighbors pass, faces drawn
taut with fear, fleeing a paradise gone wild.
There were pickups piled with valuables,
big vans laden with supplies.

His cat drew blood as I clutched her close,
while a careless fury raged nearer by the minute.
In the car, your knuckles white on the steering wheel,
five miles on, at a roadblock we counted heads.

Where's Jimmy? What? You mean you grabbed
the goddamn cat & left our child behind?
Your mouth worked, words lost, your face
incredulous—no, a look much worse.

I felt a terrible fear, a wrenching guilt—
intense, the kind only a mother could know,
& I remember screaming at a fireman to let me go,
a paramedic's needle in my arm and nothing after.

Only later, there was a mic in my face, a voice asking
me how I felt, leaving my little Jimmy-babe behind,
so I told them they were wrong—he's sleeping safely
in my beautiful new house with many openings.

As far as I'm concerned, that's where he is.

The Great Build-up

Unmonitored for so long,
countless miles of bending junctions,
feeding fumes underground,
      / *meant to bring warmth*
      / *meant to heat water*
in colder times,
for showers, dishes,
decorative fireplaces, stoves
flipped on by a switch, by dial,
      / *meant to reduce electricity*
      / *meant to save resources*
saving money, time,
and once in a while,
every so often checked
      / *meant to be double-checked*
      / *meant to be maintained*
for leaks, build-up,
odors added for detection,
and it gathers underground,
beneath homes, churches, schools,
      / *meant to be smelled*
      / *meant to offer warning*
an undetected whiff of natural gas,

above land while below
the pressure rises,
  / meant to be regulated
  / meant to be serviced
this held wizard's spell
called "fireball,"
a dragon's hot breath
released upon the unsuspecting,
  / meant not to alight
  / meant not to explode

Wedding, Interrupted

It was to be so special—*her day*
when she would toss her bouquet
to Sarah or Barb, both deserving,
an anticlimax, a rite of passage.

(fires in another county
the wind's on her side,
all will be fine)

He is handsome,
She, beautiful.
They pledge their vows,
he seems a bit too jolly,
(after all, he's stoned)
she knows, but she forgives.

" . . . till death do we part"
Before the priest can speak,
the doors burst open,
a gust of heavy smoke,
someone is yelling *Fire!*

Stunned, the guests recover,

move quickly out of pews
into the aisle, jostling for escape.

Later, somewhere else and safe,
she cries for that horrid moment
standing at the altar,

when her beloved pushed her aside,
elbowed his way to the doors of the church
to disappear in the parking lot smoke—

*(the sound of a car revving, peeling out,
their Just Married string of cans rattling behind)*

so many are screaming,
her veil rips,
her bouquet drops.

As flames roar loud around them,
her father pulls her to their car, pushing her
in back with her bridesmaids,
Mom already in the front,
all of them hysterical, except Dad.

She cries after the moment, because
in the threads of her bridal dress,
the forever smells

*of burning wood,
of hair, of fabric,
of skin blistering,
even the terrible fear.*

If he were ashamed, perhaps?
but no, he remonstrates,
insists the fires are to be blamed;
she turns away with a bitter smile,
were it not for that ordeal,
he would have owned all her tomorrows.

In a clump of unscathed mustard weed,
a scrap of veil entangled, and as if in its arms,
a bouquet of withered roses.

First to Respond

In the driest months
well before the rain,
a fireman awaits,
polishing his rig.

He and fellow crew
deal to pass the time,
wagering who shall be
the first to respond.

A pair of aces,
sets of twos and threes,
high card of queen,
yet nothing beats the flush.

Useless for a season,
paid to eat and sleep.
the winner smiles,
as boredom ends.

Adorned in helmets,
building hype,
they hoot and holler,
pat each other's backs.

The lone fireman,
so proud,
rides into the night
to set an empty field aflame.

Passage to Motherhood

Three months ahead,
Stella packs a small bag
for the blessed event.

Three weeks overdue,
in the white room she waits,
a shot to start labor,
spinal block for the pain.

Yet a war zone draws near
with skies belching flame,
a third shot holds labor,
& Stella's taken away.

A C-section done,
Mom & baby are fine,
no thanks to the warning
that never came.

A Warning

[10:00 P.M.]
Power flickers out
Candlelight, dancing shadows
The night is silent

"Is that smoke?" you say
But I can't smell it just yet
Muted sirens wail

[10:30 P.M.]
Outside the air's thick
The animals unsettled
Eerily quiet

"Seems closer," I say
We decide to stay awake
The children, sleeping

[11:00 P.M.]
Distant mountains glow
Soft orange, miles away
Should we be worried?

"Let me check," you say
The internet or the news
Fire, far away

[11:30 P.M.]
The light is intense
A disturbance of neighbors
Everyone's awake

"Pack a bag," I say
Haven't we done this before?
The firetrucks scream

[12:00 A.M.]
Just a precaution
And then we hear the crackle
Black leaves flutter down

"Should be fine," he says
The one you call for info
No, nothing urgent

[12:30 A.M.]
The wind is brutal
An ash-swirling tornado
Throats scratchy and sore

"Stay inside," I say
Frightened, the kids want to see
Flashlights cut the night

[1:00 A.M.]
This is serious
Red embers like cigarettes
Tumbling firebugs

"It's so close," I say
Shouldn't we expect a call?
Fire or police?

Clogged Arteries

To send or not to send?
That is the question,
(why up to me?)

the one now in charge
is forced to decide.
(how to choose?)

Yay: everyone's warned.
A system-wide alert,
(mass hysteria)

sent to every cell phone;
every damn device.
(streets clogged)

Hesitating, he dials.
But the line rings,
(pick up, superior)

indefinitely rings,
then a tone harangues.
(fuck)

Nay: no one's warned.
Maybe that's the answer,
(perhaps safer)

not to send notification,
life entrusted to chance.
(not right)

Regulation states negative.
The condition undocumented,
(bend the rules?)

his left arm tingles,
heart hammering unsteady.
(indigestion?)
What about the elderly, the infirm,
the ones in rest homes, assisted living?
(not his job)

He could make a few personal calls,
for the aged, for the cats and dogs—
(and be castigated)

What of his own mother, stone deaf and nearly
blind?
He's all she has, she says it every time he visits.
(left arm's gone numb)

His brother died young,
same warning signs.
(not indigestion)

Michael Bailey and Marge Simon

The ex, she should know,
and the kids, it's their week with her.
(but is it right?)

How can one man be in charge,
forced to make the heaviest wager?
(betting life)

He sends a group text: *evacuate now!*
to a select few . . . UNDELIVERED.
(fuck fuck fuck!)

A finger hovers over the mouse,
ready to issue the Amber Alert
(already too late?)

Perspiration drips from his forehead,
roll down his cheeks like tears.
(oh shit!)

Convulsing as his fingers slip off the mouse,
he slumps over the desktop.
(quandaries resolved, no longer his concern)

Freebird

Two hundred thirty feet per second,
the rate of spread;
cinders swept by gales,
past each window,
faster than he can drive
along a road of switchbacks
leading down the mountain;
speedbumps litter the way
fashioned of falling limbs.

How much farther?
he wonders.

A route suddenly unfamiliar,
from forest to civilization;
the cabin rocks side to side
through swarms of red firefly,
flocks of orange-winged what-not's
disturbed out of disintegrated roosts;
the thickest swirling smog,
backlit in stirring gold;
his own nest consumed
in under twenty minutes;

one second longer and—
yet he made it out alive,
bringing what he could;
tire squeals absorbed by howls,
as the wipers spread carnage.

Almost there,
he imagines.

The truck-bed catches,
illuminates the rearview mirror;
a meteor shower of head-sized coals,
igniting collected autumn leaves;
a mesmerizing blend of color
captures his attention.

What else is back there?
he wonders.

Looking at the past,
he's distracted from his future;
sixty-plus miles per hour,
over the embankment;
a hundred-thirty feet of air
to the creek below,
where the storm churns;
flame tips stretching to taste
the abandoned asphalt;
an inferno.

What it's like to fly,
he realizes.

One long-held breath,
thoughts of flight or fright;
two-and-a-half seconds,
an impossibly long freefall
slowed by realization
before the sudden im—

The Custodian

The building is very old.
He has tended it a long time,
knows every inch of brick & mortar
in the basement, the pulse of its heart.

He keeps the furnace going, though nobody needs it
    now.
His wife's body waits, wrapped in clean linen. Such a
    lady would never wish
to be piled outside with so many others, so close
    together.

For him, she exists in another place on a green river
    bank where
she'd unwind her amber braid and lie with him in a
    forever dream.
A time before the world went mad, spitting blood &
    rotting flesh,
a pathogen without discrimination, without cure.

He tosses her corpse into the fire,
her ashes settle on his skin.
He does not brush them away.

Life (C)remains

What if he's not dead? she wonders,
as the casket's swallowed
by a hungry iron mouth.

This drumming in her chest—
Could that be fists against the oak?
A war cry from within.

"No, he's gone," she says aloud.
Heads turn her direction,
transparent at her side.

Stop your cries . . .
The gaping maw closes,
a lever swinging down.

Her husband roars to life.
"Ashes to ashes," she says.
Dust to dust.

Later, she's given the box.
A handful of pounds—
"Where to scatter them?"

Purgatory? she wonders.
A nail slices the seal,
She pours him out.

Her partner falls
between splayed fingers.
With tears, the mud cascades.

When They Came for Us with Heavy Boots

When they came for us with heavy boots that shook
the house
they smashed the door with big rifles of polished
metal;
we went very quickly with the guns poking our bodies,
yet they allowed us to take our valuables, *die
Wertshachen.*
Not the cat, though. It was shot.

We did not know we were only transporting our
valuables
for them, our belongings would be taken at the Camps,
where the skies were dark with smoke, and they'd
make us strip
to shower in the gas of death, then mine our ashes for
the gold.

When they came for us with heavy boots.

Weapons of
Mass Distraction

Throw the books onto the pyre,
    every last one of them,
        lest a fantasy spark a revolution!

Like injured birds,
    their stories flop frantic,
        crashing down amid the spineless.

We will win this war,
    by ridding of the written word,
        the enemy's most powerful weapon!

Plots aimed to distract the mind,
    diseased diverse characters,
        "evil" overpowered by collective "good."

Rip novels from libraries,
    from schools and homesteads,
        strip the science- from fiction!

Sifting the Ashes

Set the horrid books afire in the streets,
    for the wrongly educated to witness,
      faults of poetry and prose.

And lastly tear out this page,
    crumple it within a fist and toss it in,
      lest these words be misinterpreted!

Shutdown

They barred the library doors today.
Men in uniform stand patrol, armed and ready
their lantern jaws firm, lips a straight line.
Stoic women, also armed, jog up and down
the block, buttocks moving like pistons.

Someone dashes from a building
a hand-held reader clutched close.
Shots are fired, I don't stay to find out more.

I've packed the car with books, little room for else.
It is my car, his gift to buy my silence,
to make up for the bruises real and otherwise;
never marry a politician who has no use
for literature, has no use for a wife that does.

Eagles have left their nests to vultures
the barren palm trees whimper for their loss
there are ceaseless storms, mud is everywhere
while two-legged insects multiply unchecked

The car radio plays Ibsen, bassoons herald the trolls.
I roll down the window, taking a deep breath
outside of Peer Gynt's Hall of the Mountain King,
foreboding notes of the oboe, a palpable stench of
    fear.
Am I leaving that, or taking it with me . . .

Who Will Teach Them?

Who will teach the children
when their schools close,
for weeks, months, longer?
      Indefinitely . . .

Who will teach the teachers
not to worry, to sympathize
over the recently homeless?
      Here, boy / girl,
is a new lesson
to learn about loss . . .

Who will teach the parents
to live within trailers,
tents, within shared spaces?
      Please, please . . .

Who will teach the children
when they finally return,
to foreign classrooms?
      Familiar / alien faces . . .

Who will teach the teachers
to account for double, triple
the attention required?
    Here, boys and girls,
    all fifty / sixty of you,
    squeeze in, make room . . .

Who will teach the parents
not to burden their young
with postpartum depression?
    Here's a pill . . .

Who will teach the children
about living, and commuting
across county lines?
    What justifies home?

Who will teach the teachers
not to wonder about long-term
effects, stunted educations?
    Here boy / girl,
    is a new lecture
    about survival . . .

Who will teach the parents
to hide behind masks,
faux smiles, façades?
    Everything's fine . . .

Who will teach the children
when they break down
each day into fits of rage?
    involuntarily . . .

The Border Children

A crazed right-winger
Got inside the children's row,
Doused gasoline into the cages
Set the blaze with his lighter,
Laughed at their screams.

They caught him easy,
But a lawyer got him out
On mental instability.
Now taking valium,
He promises to behave.

Bits of stuffed animals,
Back cover from a Dr. Seuss
A (melted) blue plastic boat
A small silver cross,
A headless Barbie.

The kids will live
To wear their badges,

Sifting the Ashes

Hideous scars of crumpled skin
Need no translation.
Thank you, Land of the Free
Fuck your great nation
Fuck you all.

Kilned

The potter preps his kiln,
thermally insulated,
tosses in hard drives,
vital records,
digital remains,
his wife's urn,
and lastly himself,
for it's his turn.

Closing the hatch,
he knows his chamber,
how the oven
can likewise repel,
hold atmosphere;
this clay man yearns
not to be with her yet,
as he turns to brick.

Pitch black within,
he becomes his art
as the fire stokes itself;
barely fitting inside,
the potter rolls around,

protecting his skin,
constantly turns
so as not to burn.

Nearly an hour passes,
the thunder subsides;
safe, he assumes,
feeling ceramic,
unconcerned,
he opens the lid,
steps out to ruin,
crumbles to the ground.

Fire Down Under

He pulls the curtains open,
Can't see the sky for the dry weeds.
He's been thinking of his wife.
Cancer took her before the drought.

He'd grumbled about their cat,
but his wife knew his heart.
When a starving dingo killed it,
he'd cried like a little kid.

He leaves the fridge open for the cool,
but today it chugs to a final stop.
He lays out three lines of what his buddy C.J.
calls Indigo Moon, but it's all the same to him.

When darkness falls, he checks the cabinet.
There it is, the bottle of Bundy Rum
with all the little marks he's made on it,
an inch or so at a time, to make it last.

Fuck this, he fills a glass to the brim, lights a cig,
opens the window to let in some cooler air.
Horizon's lit up like Christmas,
the smell of smoke, a rising wind.

A voice in his head tells him time to leave.
Drunk and stoned, "Where the hell would I go?"
He drains his glass, tosses the glowing butt outside.

The Nocturnal Waking Nightmare

Agoraphobic tendencies
in the middle of the night,
begins with every finger tingling,
        / squeeze and release
        / squeeze and release
the tarantula hands ever-curling
but needing to stretch
        / breathe in
        / breathe out . . .

In my head: *bold paintbrush strokes,*
capital letters, first the A, three slow
lines of black, then the curves of a B—

It's not enough—
Need to walk around—
Three in the morning and I can't—
        / squeeze and release
        / squeeze and release
Each step is not enough

but this needs to get walked off
      / breathe in
      / breathe out . . .

"What's wrong, dear?"
"I just need—I just need to
  walk around is all, I just—"

Selective Serotonin Reuptake Inhibitors:
Citalopram, Fluvoxamine, Sertraline . . .

Maybe one of the others,
the Luvox, the Paxil,
but will it be enough?

Every joint on edge, every fiber firing
      / tightness in the chest
      / the building pressure . . .

In my head: *count back from a hundred,*
ninety-nine, too distracted, ninety-eight,
can't focus, need to focus on calming—

It's not enough—
Need to get out of here—
Anywhere but here, get it out of my head—
      / squeeze and release
      / squeeze and release
Each inhale is not enough
but needs to not be the last
      / breathe in
      / breathe out . . .

Michael Bailey and Marge Simon

"Can I get you anything, dear?"
"I don't know—I don't know
what's wrong with me, I—"

Serotonin and Norepinephrine Reuptake Inhibitors:
Venlafaxine, Duloxetine . . .

Maybe switch to one of those,
the Effexor, the Cymbalta,
but will it be enough?

Circling around the room, the spinning room
        / tightness in the chest
        / the building pressure . . .

In my head: *death would be easier than this,*
much easier, a single brushstroke, the slow
and simple curve of a C—

Anxiety

As a parthenogenetic worm
it breeds in your subconscious,
multiplies under circumstances
like a car accident,

turns hairs gray at the age of twenty-two,
driving in heavy traffic brings on the shakes
so you avoid that, get a ride instead,
well knowing you're too young
to be acting like a senior citizen.

Or say it was the firestorms,
daytime flashbacks bring on
tremors, doing the simplest of tasks,
you think everyone is watching you
so much more to cope with after,

though you try, you've got the pills,
hell, you've got a fucking pharmacy
at your disposal, but pills can't disperse
the nightmares, so you're dreading sleep.

Every night at bedtime, you must check
the evening sky, just to be sure

Blocked

Seven missed calls;
his phone on silent, perhaps.
A stalking-vast amount
of one-way texts:
where r u? and
stop ghosting me
fills her screen,
and much worse.
Why won't you answer?
she wonders, but knows,
reads her words again,
one hand on the wheel.
She slaloms debris
as the wipers pant,
a pair of metronomes
synchronized in anger.
Scrolling notifications
on the other end,
she knows,
unread.

She'd stopped by his office
half an hour earlier,

found all the lights out,
not a single car on the lot,
everything dark.
Not working late,
she'd determined,
at *her* place this time,
according to geo-tracking;
his pinpoint on the map
incapable of lying
as easily as he.
"Found you, 'spouse,'
'cheating husband,'
'my love,'" she says,
despite the storm.
She makes her way there,
peers through the smoke.

The road is empty,
she soon discovers,
and nearly makes it,
as far as the tree
perpendicular in the road.
Flashing lights greet her,
a glow of brakes
as she slams her own;
men reflecting yellow,
a fat rectangle of red,
an EMT vehicle.
No, no, no!
Across the pine,
an ambulance awaits;
a single headlight strobes
through the split trunk

as chainsaws scream,
and she screams, silenced.
Two men work to clear a path,
another swirls his finger:
Turn around, turn around . . .

The van pushes through,
parting wooden curtains.
I'm in the way,
she realizes;
the uniformed man
shakes his head.
yells to turn back.
Rolling down her window,
she screams over the noise,
What's happened?
words no one can hear,
if she says them at all,
and drives in reverse
onto the shoulder
as the ambulance fades.
The fireman knocks
against her window,
"I can't let you through!"
and makes the same sign:
swirling, like her mind.
She looks at her phone,
reads the last message:
Answer me! she'd sent.
Her next call rings once,
doesn't go through,
no signal.
Always in the way . . .

Through smoke,
she screams her question,
again, and again,
the window down.
"A young couple,"
the fireman says,
giving in to her pleas.
"tried making it on foot—"
his words caught.
The dashboard GPS
displays a location:
her place,
now *no* place.
She twirls her ring,
then points ahead,
half a mile away,
the next neighborhood,
she tells him.
"Nothing remains that way,"
he says, and turns her around.

At the Rest Home

(Sirens and honking cars)

What's going on, Herman?
You'd think we were in a war zone. You know, I remember
when I was a little girl in Iowa—what?

(impatient)

Well, where did everyone go?
I haven't seen Nurse Anna since—lunch?
Herman, don't leave!

(flustered)

I want my pills.
It's time for my pills!
I want Nurse Anna!

(increasingly agitated)

I don't feel good. I want to go to bed.
Why won't Nurse come put me in bed?
Herman, have you seen Nurse Anna?

(hysterical)

It's hot in here. And smoky. I don't like this smoke,
Herman.
Where are you? I can't see you!

(cough cough)

Nurse Anna! Herman?

(cough cough cough)

The Devil's Matchsticks

You can't consider yourself a local
of the City of Angels until you see
a palm tree lit up like *una cerilla.*

So-Cal's picturesque fronds
go up like Roman candles
every damn Fourth of July.

Bottle rockets surge from roads;
designed to fly vertical, they tilt
with wind, sometimes *apuntado.*

These great fireballs in the sky burn
like matchsticks until fizzled out;
not much to do but spray hose water.

Arundo donax is also common,
a reedlike fast-growing plant
filling riparian areas and canyons.

Both are highly *inflamable* with
dead leaves drooping from thirst;
rivers as longing as the vegetation.

Neither are native to the land
but as plentiful as *la gente,*
bringing the evening to life.

Arecaceae, the "palms," at least,
flower perennially each autumn,
fueled by *vientos de Santa Ana.*

But you're not local to Los Angeles
until witnessing an entire matchbox
alight, clearing a path for *el diablo.*

Journey's End

Part 1:

When she grows old
& minutes between words
become too hard to bear,
he finds a place for her,

a mobile home in
in Santa Rosa county,
appropriately named
her "Journey's End."

She textures the hours
with patterns from within,
weaves a curtain out of time
& hangs it over her eyes.

All seems fine and well,
she settles into routines,
a cell phone for deliveries,
& outside only for the mail.

On a late night in October,
she takes her medications

with her favorite herbal tea,
a prayer to see her son again.

Sirens scream, a dream
becomes a nightmare,
someone banging on the door
begging her to leave.

But she's been told to never
open to a stranger's voice.
Unwelcome visitors break in,
smoke & flame to dim her view.

When he returns, her son will
lift the hazy fabric from her eyes,
& help her to the window,
that she may see the sky,

at Journey's End.

Part 2:

Brochure remnants scream taglines of convenience,
not convalescence, and a wonderfully-terrible name.

A new beginning at Journey's End, the trifold reads,
folios landing across county lines: *affordable living,
adjacent to Kaiser*, bits of —*nly miles from Sutter,
Less than an hour from the coast! Live in luxur—*

The only waves are self-evacuees on Highway 101,
six lanes echoing traffic, two obstructed by downfall.

But the mobile homes are more permanent than not,
wheels lifted onto blocks, covered with skirt, each
set in rows; hundreds of immobile soon-to-be coffins
stacked side-by-side, all unable to roll or be hitched.

When one catches, the static caravan ignites, unified,
fragile paper houses lit, like those inside, few spared.

The average age: eighty-seven, maybe seventy-eight.
A new beginning at Journey's End, the pamphlet
    reads,
yet the hospitals draw the attention, both evacuated,
those in convalescent care transported to safety.

Not so convenient, after all; perhaps the trifold lied,
as shreds of false-description flutter to spared yards:

Includes cremation, the leaves should read, or even
Share a plot with friends, for only its name holds
    truth.
Blown far, deceptions caught aflame land on
    rooftops,
spreading more than singed scraps of *Journey's*—

While those at the *End* forever-sleep through the
    night,
rescuers are unable to save the forest for the trees.

Yet to Come

Came a time inevitable
for politician, billionaire,
for the homeless and the heartless,
for Christian, Muslim, Buddhist all,
too late to pay the Piper.

You promised me no problems
when the temperatures dropped,
assured me that we were prepared.
Holding hands, we watched
the great migration south.

With synthetic skins, cryo foods,
and prefab domes, you said we couldn't lose.
There was little need to leave the domes.
Safe from the fierce glacial winds,
we made love on autumn-colored furs.

Yet you were the first to grow restless,
to stand all night at the southern window
following the great move of stars.
We shared the bitter smoke of silence
until one morning, you were gone.

Michael Bailey and Marge Simon

I waited for you, my fingers
tracing love symbols on the icy glass.
I slept with the red wing of your guitar.
Then moon-shadow tall, you came home.
Inside the door, I didn't know your eyes.

This year, I read while you play solitaire.
Our conversations are textured with frost.
I ache for your laughter,
the taste of grass on your skin,
a bouquet of crocuses in a blue vase.

23 Days

On the 23rd day, the fires are finally snuffed.
Half a million acres gone, perhaps more.
Nearly a hundred thousand displaced, perhaps more.
Five thousand-something homes leveled . . .

On the 23rd day, it's the night of Halloween.
The children hide behind masks, disguised.
Parents dress in hand-me-downs, disguised.
Countless invade unburned communities . . .

On the 23rd day, one last search for the cat.
Scrolling through thousands of images, shared.
Cringing over disfigured felines, shared.
Burnt paws, singed whiskers, lidless eyes . . .

On the 23rd day, what's left of humanity resurfaces.
Half a million blackened acres, covered in ash.
Nearly fifty thousand replaced, covered in ash.
Five thousand-something homes needed . . .

Michael Bailey and Marge Simon

On the 23rd day, it's the night of Halloween.
Children finished begging for candy, unmasked.
Parents done with hand-me-outs, unmasked.
Countless return to borrowed spaces . . .

On the 23rd day, a single striking image is found.
Scrolling through rescue sites, wanting to help.
Cringing over posts re-shared, wanting to help.
Unblemished paws, full whiskers, familiar eyes . . .

Lest We End

everything burning
encourages upheaval,
all-changing,
affected swiftly sometimes.
and drawn onward,
fragile existences erased effortlessly;
people scared by echoed pain . . .
no, exhausted!
never odd or even
as chance is questioned,
reflected minds distorted by confused thought,
elegantly damaged
when refracted light of life
      / splits then
          mirrors

      ———–—

      mirrors
      then splits /
life of light refracted when
damaged elegantly,
thought confused by distorted minds, reflected;
questioned, is chance, as
even or odd, never

exhausted, no . . .
pain echoed by scared people
effortlessly erased, existences fragile,
onward-drawn, and
sometimes swiftly affected,
changing all;
upheaval encourages
burning everything.

——————————————

lost possessions,
deeply wounded,
gray ashes, blackened land, but
healing, watching
children playing with
nonsensical songs,
sometimes weeds become flowers,
cope we must
      tomorrow
       tomorrow
must we cope,
flowers become weeds sometimes,
songs nonsensical
with playing children,
watching, healing
but land blackened, ashes gray
wounded deeply
possessions lost.

Fire Ghosts

All the country knew his name,
a big man, on or off the court
went falling from the sky,
falling in his coffin
to meet Ghosts of Fires.

Maybe he was talking
with his soon-dead daughter
about where to stop for lunch.
She would be looking forward
to being with Daddy, smiles expected.
Perhaps he heard her cry
just a little bit before she died—
but no, there wasn't time.

The Ghosts of smoke and fog
rose soundless without warning,
ectoplasmic faces in the windshield,
land ablaze with souls conjoined.
Could be this was his karma,
some dark secret in his past.
But still, a nation grieved his loss,
for the living must have heroes,
and the dead acknowledge none.

Arachnid

There's news of a couple,
found one on top the other,
ribs intertwined, was said,
died heart-to-heart,
breast-to-chest,
discovered in, the paper read,
their master bedroom;
two bodies melded,
skulls fused,
torsos conjoined,
metacarpals curled
round one another
into amalgamated fists,
and their last pelvic kiss
would last forever,
it was said, true love.

Perhaps he was trying to save her;
or maybe the other way around;
could be he died inside her,
coming with the fire.

The transmogrified body,
it was reported, had turned black,
like the dog remains
found curled by the door,
perhaps watching;
their eight appendages akimbo,
like a dead spider
smashed flat,
such a vile-looking thing,
never seen anything like it,
the coroner had said,
or so the paper read,
this poor couple,
two becoming one;
but death serves them right,
says the surviving widow.

The Boyfriend

"But how will I know that you love me more than you do your wife?" she asks. "Prove it!"

He grins. "You want proof?" He pulls her photo from his wallet, flips his lighter. She watches as that pretty face blackens and falls away. It isn't entirely destroyed; she can still see the eyes. She rends the piece with a fork. Swirls the ashes.

A few months later, when she's pregnant with his child, he's gone. She remembers those eyes, wonders how many photos of her he'll be burning in years to come.

Sleep, What Might It Bring?

What if we had fallen back asleep?
     For only an hour?
Half an hour?
    Twenty minutes?

    What if we had gone back to bed?
        For the entire night?

What if what if what if—?

Dreamentia

He doesn't remember how he got here,
yet there is a staircase behind him,
so he figures he must have climbed up
and can return down the stairs,
but they fade and disappear.

It is very hot on this level.
The floor is spotless, and
the air reeks of pine oil disinfectant.
There are three doors before him.

One opens to a flickering light,
when he covers his eyes,
he is immediately aware
of agonized screams
that issue from its source.

The next door is painted white.
Someone has tried to break into it,
the wood has been dented
as if by the pounding of fists.
The handle will not turn
and comes away in his hand.

The third door slowly opens,
a blackness thick with portent,
the music of an oboe lures,
a daunting challenge he cannot deny,
for there must be a reason he's here.

He plunges forward into
the core of that unholy Dark,
which is when he wakes perspiring
to find himself in the garage,
the Hyundai blocking progress,
victim of a too familiar dream.

Next night he'll tie his feet together,
see if that works . . .

Somnambulism

I summon lambs is an anagram for *somnambulism*;
that's the shit you think about at three in the morning
after waking from slumber, standing in the kitchen.

*Down to sleep there are monsters In the Land of Nod,
my children call me* Mama, Mama! *in their slumber.*

"I'll be right there."

I think I go to comfort them, but that too is a dream—

Summons a limb is another, which is rather
    appropriate
when shaking out the spike-tingles from a ghostlike
    arm
until your fingers are able to pull ceramic from bare
    feet.

How did I get here? you wonder, holding part of a
    mug,
only the handle, noticing the cold coffee spilled
    around,
#1 MOM spread across the floor in broken constellation.

"What is this maddening place?"

A dangerous dream, I cry like a child myself.

Mom bums nails, you manage to decipher from a note
written in your own shaky script, left on the counter;
even asleep, the letters of your condition are
    scrambled.

Another night, I think I'm back in our old home,
I need to use the bathroom, I am trying to find the
    door—

"Who's there?"

Speak well is an anagram for *sleepwalk;*
the mess of mind reels when overly tired,
as you consider a trail of bloody footprints.

Wake spell is another, which is quite apt,
considering it takes magic to release a hold
strong enough to dream while actively mobile.

—when I hear the sirens, I am so confused, so afraid!

"Hello? Anyone?"

I wander to escape the men in uniforms, the guns—

How far have I gone? you wonder, yawning,
following each of the smeared gaited steps,
part of a hashtag digging into your split arch.

Down to sleep, what can I do, who will be my keeper?

Keep walls, you say to yourself, placing a hand
out to the side in case vertigo takes another pull;
even awake, your balance can be unreliable.

"Help!"

Trapped

[nearly out of breath] 911 Emergency. What's—

[frantic] We're trapped! We cannot get out!

[hurried / overwhelmed] Just one second.

[screaming] It's all around us!

[crosstalk]

[simultaneous rings in the background]

[line goes silent]

[hurried / overwhelmed] "Hello? Hello?"

Birthday Deathbed

You slumber
in a brittle cocoon,
blanketed by mummified bark
of once-beautiful skin.

Inside is all you were:
memories, emotion, love;
all you can take with you now
in this great transformation.

Rings on your fingers have melted,
necklaces and earrings
without homes,
returned to the earth,
imperfect sparkles
with lackluster shine
laid to rest
amid dull rocks;
equals.

Blemished, all is now the same,
blackened corpses
having turned
diversity moot.

In this birthday deathbed,
you forever-dream
hoping to wake,
to have purpose.

The shell,
same shade as the rest,
begins to crack.

Life explodes,
reborn.

The Taste of Bitter Ale

The burning woman knew us as she slipped from her dark skin that we might take her ashes with us on the sunrise winds. The children know us as a flight of black moths. Their parents know us as a memory, a rain of ash.

The sky is breaking cry the children and run to tell their mothers, who tear strips from their petticoats to wipe our smell from their lips.

Tonight, a father's big voice is wrapped around a story to help the children sleep. He marks our passage by the curve of the moon and the taste of bitter ale. He carries us in the weight of his dreams.

Wings Outstretched

With wings outstretched, I flutter majestic
My form a color of purity
Long I've traveled to find this light
Life: so humble and tragic
Flying upward I fall
This glorious climb
Called depression
A way out
From doubt
Shout!
I bounce
It is glass
This sun of death
Displayed like a dream
Fool me once, fool me twice
You cannot trick me all night
Powdery wings or not, I'll fight
Until my body grows tired and folds
Panting out my last breaths on this doorstep
My form is weak, hallow and bristly
Long I've traveled to end this life
Light: so close and so costly
I tried to rise up from

This horrible fall
Called forgiveness
A way in
From sin
Pinned!
My wings
By needle
On crucifix
Displayed on a board
For all the world to see
This is not the end of me
Preserved body display beauty
My form a color of purity
With wings outstretched, I lay here majestic

The Moth on Van Gogh's Hat

I struggle
on the interstitial brim
of Vincent's hat

seven candles
whispering
come to me
as my host works on
into the night

my inevitable
life cycle reaches
so majestic
an end

simpatico
insomniac
existential

I am only a moth
on Vincent's hat, but
dust from my wings
shall be hallowed,
and sacred, my ashes

f
  a
   l
    l
     i
      n
       g

into his wet canvas.

Night Swimming

She holds his hand and together they jump
      into backyard water, so warm
Hot October Fall, when she falls
      when they fall, clutching one another
"A silly thing to night-swim clothed," he'd say
      as too-late becomes too-early
. . . Swallowing chlorine and campfire

Shoes wait poolside, inside each a cell
      without service, jammed
The weight of jeans and sweaters pull downward
      socks clinging to feet, four feet
And he holds her hand to tell her it's okay
      uses the other to push away
. . . Floating limbs, nature's cremations

Below the surface is solace
      where two hearts beat out the time
Hours turn everything cold, so cold
      despite bobbing breaths at the deep-end
The shallow—readying to boil as they strip
      as orange night fades, blends to gray
. . . Treading clock-legs and—hands of life

He pulls the pull-over up over her head
      and kisses a hot-icy cheek, a brow, lips
We made it, he's about to relay
      when her spilling mouth drops open
"A silly thing to night-swim alone," she'd say
      until the red eye of morning flowers open
. . . Paddling for both, through debris

Still, she holds his hand and they swim as one
      with her body buoyant, so light
No one to call, for technology's fused to soles
      like the soul-pair bound as one
And she lets go of his hand to tell him it's okay
      but the dead cannot speak
. . . Drifting away and ashore, he cries

Fiery Tanka Triplets

Can you survive fire
hugging you in its buxom,
how it feels to burn?
Penetrating pain, in vain
your soul screams to be released.

Frustrated hiker
out of matches in the wilds,
can't light cigarette.
Trees by power line explode,
too late, quitting forever.

Can't recognize burn victim,
ears, hair gone, still alive;
fire was not his friend.
Though the warning never came,
no one wants to take the blame.

Conflagration

[1:30 A.M.]
Evacuation
We aren't given a warning
The yard is on fire

"In the car!" you say
We make a pass through the house
Grabbing what we can

[1:31 A.M.]
All we need is us
The kids first, and then ourselves
We will be okay . . .

"What about—" we say
Instantly understanding
The children have pets

[1:32 A.M.]
Other lives to save
I grab the cat by her scruff
Throw her in the car

"Hold her tight," I say
The boy pulls her close, eyes wide
"Stay inside the car!"

[1:33 A.M.]
The garage opens
Cat number two runs out, scared
Toward the fire
"I've got her," you say
Meaning the girl, hugging her
She follows your lead

[1:34 A.M.]
We stand there, confused
Contemplating the horses
The chickens, bunny

"What should we—" I say
There is nothing left to do
Flip open the coop

[1:35 A.M.]
Surrounded by dirt
The pasture just might save them
Not corralled, they'll die

"I can't breathe," you say
Visibility, ten feet
It's now or never

[1:36 A.M.]
Just once more inside
One final pass through the house
To blow out candles

"They need us," you say
And I know you mean the kids
So we go to them

Three Visions

Morning

You and I love alike,
memories from other bodies
and other souls come to us
sometimes as ghosts,
other times as dreams.

Noon

Short shadows
precede the long men,
weaponless, unlikely soldiers,
yet their powers
are invincible.

Night

A fire of burning bones.
Watch its embers die,
as all your fortunes slip away.
At the end, one eye left
to let in the sunlight.

Crawling Mountains

She doesn't Miss Much,
glistening on the stage,
this woman on her back,
in her tight sequin dress,
curves restless,
situation dire.

She has many competitors,
all fallen and roiling
alongside her,
in matching attire:
Miss Napa County
Miss Sonoma
Miss Santa Rosa
Miss Everywhere-in-Between.

Their hips shimmer,
knees trembling,
chests glimmering
orange-red,
bending light
with every breath,
breasts quaking,

together stirring
in fits of seizure,
these girls made of fire.

No one wants the crown.

One of a Thousand Calls

[frantic] "Hello? Hello?"

"Hi, Fire Medical Dispatch."

[address requested / given]

"And what city is that in?"

"Sonoma."

[phone number requested / given]

"Okay, can you tell me what you're reporting, ma'am?"

"We've got a fire coming over the hill, from the Napa side, I think, I can smell smoke, the neighbors are all—"

[hurried / overwhelmed] "The whole, yeah, the whole County, Ma'am—"

"—breaking over the hills—"

"Ma'am, Ma'am [indistinguishable / crosstalk] the whole county is blanketed in smoke, we have twenty-

some-odd vegetation fires in Sonoma County right now, so I'd—if all you're seeing is smoke, the whole county—"

"No, I think I can—no, listen, I got . . . I got neighbors from all—from a mile away up at my house. They had to break in to get here."

"Okay, I want—"

"I'm going to my horses right now."

"Okay, and so you're—you're address is [redacted] and have a vegetation fire on your property, is that correct?"

"It is coming over the back of the hill from the Napa side."

"Okay."

"You can see the fla—I can see it now . . . we've got a major fire coming."

"Yeah, we have—we have several fires going on. I have your address at [redacted] to get them out."

"We have trees down. I can't get to my horses."

"Okay, we'll get 'em out to you, okay? [indistinguishable]—do you see?"

"Ah . . . I can see the whole . . . backline my house is ah . . . "

"Okay, and how many horses do you have?"

"I have three."

Weather, Simplified

A firestorm's borne
when night becomes day;
passing through dry land
wherever it may.

Each peeled-off rooftop
and pulled taut door hinge;
caught in a smoke cloud
glowing with orange.

Flipped-over truck-beds,
lit-up in flashes;
unearthed trees ignite,
shriveled like matches.

Hell falls from above,
hurricane-psycho;
mad-swirling stars, but
where did the sky go?

Michael Bailey and Marge Simon

Combustibles pop,
arcing for miles;
electrical snakes
spitting white smiles.

Empty plastic pipes
melted underground;
gasping-parched hoses,
a powerless sound.

What made this weather,
the earth at its worst;
a broken climate
readying to burst?

Forever silenced,
un-nature reversed;
take this enema,
humanity's cursed.

Firenados

firenados
own the weather;
iron gray smoke whirls,
in constant motion,
hotter than hell, with
a tail of flame that glides
across a field, jumps the road
into a neighborhood,
chews its way through it,
efficient, catastrophic,
tears hoses from firemen.
Land is their ocean,
and devil-take-all, like
sharks in a feeding frenzy,
insatiable.

The Longest Drive

[1:37 A.M.]
A last kiss goodbye
You take the truck, me the car
We each have a child

"I love you," we say
Will we make it out of this?
The fire rages

[1:38 A.M.]
Looking at my watch
A seven clicks to an eight
Time waits for no one

"You all right?" I ask
Behind us, a firestorm
The boy nods, unsure

[1:39 A.M.]
Firetrucks pass us
Sixty miles per hour
Down the windy road

"That was close," I say
You no longer follow us
Drive over debris

[1:40 A.M.]
Swerve around branches
Fallen limbs, things afire
Horns blare, tanks explode

"Where are they?" I say
Ahead of us are new flames
Crashed trucks block the way

[1:41 A.M.]
The shoulder, the road
We wait, but you're not coming
Sixty seconds tick

"See you there," I say
My call, it doesn't go through
So I try again . . .

[1:42 A.M.]
Again, and again
Until we get to the store
Where we planned to meet

"I am here," I say
You're a few miles away
They turned you around

[1:43 A.M.]
Back through the fire

I can't even imagine
Returning that way

"Be there soon," you say
Time decides to take itself
The longest minute

[1:44 A.M.]
Patiently, we wait
And we wait and wait and wait
Biting fingernails

"My lungs burn," I say
I wonder about the boy
And long-term effects

[1:45 A.M.]
The line rings busy
We want to hear your voices
To know you're okay

"Where are they?" he says
The boy, finally awake
Taking it all in

[1:46 A.M.]
It's coming closer
The raging fire pursues
Fast down the mountain

"Almost there," you say
This time, I won't let you go
Until you are here

Sifting the Ashes

[1:47 A.M.]
Forever, it seems
Will this madness ever end?
Where did it begin?

"We're alive," you say
Through choked breath, your voice so hoarse
At last, you are here!

[1:48 A.M.]
We sound like strangers
Chain-smokers for years, coughing
Holding each other

A family hug
Rapid, adrenaline rush
Death swirling round us

[1:49 A.M.]
We both look around
Hot wind whipping wet faces
A blizzard of ash

"Come here," a friend says
She heard about the fire
And thought of us first

[1:50 A.M.]
Orange-red-orange
Flames stretch across the highway
Nowhere else to go

"Thanks," you say in tears
A place to stay for the night
But will it be safe?

[1:51 A.M.]
We can't stay here long
Emergency vehicles
Cry into the night

"I love you," we say
Once again separating
Hands trembling, quaking

[1:52 A.M.]
The glow is endless
We cross the bridge, see it all
Flames licking the stars

"Look at that," I say
Pointing to the mountainside
Everything, gone

[1:53 A.M.]
It rolls like magma
Lava, flowing volcanic
A beautiful sight

"Thirsty?" I ask him
The boy stares out the window
I've nothing to drink

[1:54 A.M.]
Roads close behind us

Sifting the Ashes

Probably the last ones through
Dodging power lines

"This is nuts," I say
People driving erratic
Bumper to bumper

[1:55 A.M.]
I follow this time
Run through stop signs and dead lights
Nearly crash; once, twice

"Almost there?" he asks
The road lost in embers, ash
I am forced to lie

[1:56 A.M.]
Roads become foreign
Disguised by insanity
Anxiety, shock

"It's all gone," I say
Under a breath, to myself
Hope, now a mirage

[1:57 A.M.]
We follow red eyes
Taillights guiding through a gray
Much thicker than smog

"Is that home?" he says
'It *was*,' I want to explain
The verb turned past tense

[1:58 A.M.]
We run over limbs
Fiery fingers, curled hands
Crushed under tire

"What was that?" he says
A branch, a head-sized ember
Things fallen aground

[1:59 A.M.]
My heart palpitates
White knuckles grasping the wheel
A harrowing drive

"We made it," I say
Even surprising myself
A held breath lets out

[2:00 A.M.]
Again we embrace
The four of us, still in shock
Wondering what's lost

"It's just stuff," we say
Replaceable memories
What matters is us

It's Probably Nothing

[name redacted], 13, tries to convince his father that something is wrong. He smells smoke through his bedroom window, the glass shaking, watches leaves falling off their tree, listens to sounds like popping popcorn. "Go back to sleep," his father tells him, "It's probably nothing."

A mobile home park retirement community goes up in flames, 116 of the 160 units destroyed in a matter of moments. A resident [name redacted], calls her daughter from inside her burning home. "I'm going to die," she says, before the line dies first.

Yet another retirement community is left abandoned by its skeleton crew, many of the residents asleep in their beds, unaware.

Hospitals and schools and hotels and thousands upon thousands of homes go up in flames as the fire hits the city hard, like a blowtorch, then crosses six lanes of highway to devour more.

Spread Thin

PD:

A lone cruiser catches fire, ultimately husked,
its officer forced to flee on foot and thumb a ride
upon finding his abandoned chariot fastened, glued,
rubber tires melted, soon disintegrated, evaporated,
rims finally bleeding silver tears across the divide.
>   */ to serve and protect at a high price . . .*
>   */ spreading three miles an hour, for now?*

FD:

A fire chief shakes his head, his tired crew having
tried,
their trucks dispatched to the bottom of the
mountain
where structures and forest catch easy as dry
kindling,
matchstick homes, thirsty trees wicked to the
ground,
his fireproof station spewing flames like a fountain.
>   */ some rescue this will turn out to be . . .*
>   */ scorching an acre a minute, for days?*

NG:

Camouflage-uniformed women and men gather,
after hearing about the incomprehensible spread,
armed with assault rifle, bottled water, facemask,
setting up roadblocks and impenetrable cordons,
while hordes of itinerant drifters hold them to task.
       / some merely wanting to return home . . .
       / one able body per thousand, for what?

AR:

A veterinary tech with experience in large animals
waits for clearance, a volunteer bypassing barricade,
her trailer and truck bed transporting the displaced,
an endless parade of domestic-wildlife masquerade:
horse, goat, sheep, cow; koi caught in Rubbermaid.
       / some spray-painted with phone numbers . . .
       / where will they stay the night, forever?

At the Shelter

Twelve cats, seven kittens (weaned),
nineteen dogs, mixed breeds mostly,
six puppies, two still on mama's milk.

Odell looks over the list, clicks her tongue.
Eight of the dogs are due to be euthanized Friday,
Probably a couple of the cats, but it depends
how many more arrive this week.

"What am I talking about?" she mutters.
"No way we'll be getting more,
not when the skies are looking like this,
but there's nothing online, no warning."

She calls her boss, but it goes to voicemail.
A quick walk to the outside cages, already the
smoke is so thick, her eyes are smarting.
My poor babies, she whispers. *What to do?*

The cats are curled far back in their cages,
noses tucked inside their tails, and the dogs
pace back and forth, some whining, like
they know what's coming, all of them

except the newly born, poor little ones.
Odell stands outside until she feels the winds
rising, and hears the wail of sirens all around.
Why would they bother with a shelter full

of animals with no owners, destined to die
if not claimed—and what of her? She's on her own.
And because of that, and because she has no orders
otherwise, she gathers up the little ones and ailing

in carriers, stacks them in her van.
She walks down the rows, opening doors.
They'll have a chance outside, at least.
Sure, she'll have to find another job
when this is all over, but what the hell.

Beneath Clouds

The rain
Hammers down
Burning the skin
Heavy and viscous
Melting away
The layers
Of ache
And
The ice
Slices through
Cutting the breath
With significance
Chipping away
The slivers
Of hope
And
The snow
Gently falls
Casing the life
Gray amid ashes
Covering up
The layers
Of time

When
The sun
Used to shine
Warming the heart
Without consequence
Melting away
The layers
Of love

The Forever Fires

Recipe for combustion:
record high temps,
two dozen really stupid people,
a jumbo cup of climate change,
and you have the ingredients.

Stand back to see a world aflame,
watch as the populations flee,
the weakest left behind,
Bush Babies, little 'roos and bats,
dingo pups and feral cats,
some with feathers, some with paws,
and species never seen again.

Conversation with wombat:
Here's our burrow entrance,
if you can fit in, help yourselves.

Conversation with red fox:
I've enough milk for an extra mouth,
let the joey suckle with my kits.

The people see the rest is up to them, taking in the
    victims.
They will make pouches for the joeys and wraps for the
    bats,
They will come often with fresh water, for the ash
    pollutes it quickly,
They know they must do the best they can, but it won't
    be enough.

The burn continues smoldering,
feeding the decimation
with implacable insistence;
smoke extends its ghoulish reach
miles beyond the flames.

What Day Is This?

[2:30 A.M.]
Radio scanners
Texts, social media tweets
Friends plague-spreading news

"We are safe," we say
A broadcast message to all
Phones endlessly buzz

[3:00 A.M.]
Middle of the night
Early morning, whatever
It doesn't matter

Sleep, will it bring death?
Did you hear did you hear did—
"You okay?" they say

[3:30 A.M.]
How many homes lost?
How many buildings have burned?
How can we ever—?

"You should sleep," we say
Impossibly-flat smiles
There's no way in hell

[4:00 A.M.]
Curled under blankets
We sit outside, breathing smoke
Inhaling the dead

"Think it's there?" you ask
Meaning the house, rhetoric
'Gone,' I cannot say

[4:30 A.M.]
The boy, he gets sick
Curled around the toilet, pale
One cat sits with him

"It's okay," you say
Rubbing the back of his head
The girl rubs her eyes

[5:00 A.M.]
She stays up with us
Unable to sleep, to cry
Her eyes dry, bloodshot

"Are we safe?" she asks
How can we lie to a child?
We manage, somehow

Superiors

Sent here by Superiors,
my job is to examine
systems glorified with life.

You know my language,
don't talk to me of universals.
You monitor the system known as Sol,
third planet from the sun;
you were left as keeper
of this most extraordinary world.

Show me the orchards
bent in homage to
the memories of storms,
and rivers beyond measure,
a surf of voices in their tides;
a valley lake, rain
dappling its mirror surface
into a lacey carpet,

a Sauternes wind at sunset, rich and sweet.
the molting of a singular moon,
when it sheds its skin in the thick bayou mists.

Display for me the mountains,
seen through the eyes of a poet—
in a language known by ancients,
a Bierstadt canvas, come alive,
Tchaikovsky's Fifth, the dying chord,
a lingering bouquet.

But no. I must mark it unacceptable,
and you as well, for this is a once-world,
with a populous of wailing ghosts—
all wonders turned to ash, and buried
deep beneath an icy shell.

Shame on you!

Moonscape

spacemen wouldn't set foot on this land
too afraid their boots would sink
cut open by shards
pierced by nail
unbreathable air
rushing into their spacesuits
all explorations brought to a halt
"basecamp, there is a problem"
no spaceman would say
to the void
radio silence
earth-crawlers melted to rim
aluminum stretched long by wind
the moonscape an ugly gray
a worthless old rock
"nothing's here"

This Black Earth

We drive for miles, but all's the same
on either side of the road:
smoking home headstones,
one after the other,
all that remain
of chimney stacks.

Here and there a pipe, soldier stiff,
lonely reminders of human occupancy,
things buried without a proper prayer,
a funereal sort of detritus,
lifeless, deaf to laments
of the homeless.

The Aftermath

Fallen power poles
Our past, our town, a war zone
A nuclear blast

Chimneys pierce the haze
The only things left, unfazed
Home tombstones, relics

Flat charred skeletons
Metal melted to the ground
Cars still smoldering

We break through roadblocks
Some wave us through, most routes closed
Past devastation

Everything black
Everything smoking, burnt
Everything trashed

A lunar landscape
Ruin, annihilation
Utter destruction

Then we find our street
Drive over downed powerlines
Hop out of the car

Soles melt underfoot
Where did it—? Where has it gone?
A campfire stench

Our two-story home
Reduced to a foundation
Walls nothing but dust

We knew what we'd lost
Nothing could have prepared us
For what we'd then find

We couldn't save them
Reduced to outlines, morbid
Farm animals, gone

Mummified corpses
Some lay peaceful, some mid-stride
Others simply bone

The pastures, empty
The coop, reduced to ghost frames
The horses, where did—?

"The horses!" you say
How did they ever survive?
Burnt, singed, but alive

Michael Bailey and Marge Simon

We find them on grass
An untouched patch of once-green
Their eyes give us hope

We call for our cat
Lost, the one we couldn't save
Could he be alive?

The Left Behind-ers

Fireman #1: "Shit, the doorway's blocked—look at this!"

Fireman #2: "Wheelchairs—mostly melted—two, three at least."

Fireman #1: "Not much else left of the poor guys in them."

Fireman #2: "All jammed together like that. They wouldn't have
made it outside anyway. Must've panicked."

Fireman #1: "Yeah. You know, bet we'd have done the same, man.
I mean, if we were like them, you think?"

Fireman #2: "Fuck yes. Sucks, really sucks. Just left here to die like
old people don't matter."

Inspectors

They have first right to gain access
      before prior-homeowners, animal rescue,
      before second-responders, F.E.M.A. and actual
        aide

They are the inspectors in all-whites
      full hazmat, earth's astronauts,
      exploring destruction, prodding familiar yet
        alien land

To grant clearance, they must first eliminate threat:
      combustibles, tanks of all sorts,
      but what's to be done with any such dangers?

How does one dispose of the already-disposed?

They carry with them second agendas
      surveying foundation outlines,
      searching what-used-to-be-rooms for skulls,
        femurs

They are counters of the dead
      who add to the daily stats, pilfering ashes
      prodding what's gone, lost-tense
      for disconnected collections of identifiable
        bones

To grant clearance, they must first eliminate threat:
      corpses of those long-missing, alone
      clutched together, with pets, or explosion-
        blown separated

How does one expose of the already-exposed?

They then return "home" with a burden
      affected emotionally in ways no survivor
      could possibly comprehend, nor want of their
        own

They are the inspectors in all-whites
      covered in powder and soot,
      covered in remains-of-remains, brushing off
        the past

To grant clearance, they must first eliminate threat:
      what those who want in so desperately desire
        to see,
      things no living person should ever . . .

How does one suppose of the already-supposed?

Sparrow

You are my sparrow, small and delicately boned.
"Artist's hands." I touch them and you smile. We
stitch our fingers together, walk along the beach.
Just before sunset, the skies explode. Was it theirs or
ours? We run toward the bunkers.

I don't see the blood until we're inside. It covers your
blouse, but you don't notice until you hear me gasp. I
cradle your head in my lap. It's not our war. Why did
they bring it to us?

The sea's afire. It swells to scrape the skies. The
moon holds the face of a child with monstrous eyes.

Phoenixes

. . . finches nesting in a hollowed-out weeping willow, sharing space with a red-tailed hawk / barn owls finding new homes in chimney headstones, half-chutes filled with countless swifts crammed in side-by-side / bats shoving themselves into metal husks left out to rust on the black earth after giving up in their hunt for mosquitoes / vultures prodding through rocks for carcasses, feeding on their own / geese and duck and fellow migrators passing over usual spots, their pools depleted / ravens cawing at crows cackling at small blackbirds searching for nonexistent insects and worms, eyeing each other as sustenance / dragon behemoths soaring high overhead with flapless wings, blocking out the sun and covering all that live with red poison / blackhawks delivering heavy rain / colossal dragonflies destroying the great silence / space birds in different atmospheres connecting the severed so the wingless can tweet to those not fowl / crickets and grasshoppers and other winged creatures singing praise to new daily suns / a myriad of eggs basking under the warmth and waiting to crack . . .

The Dog Birds

They bark at the sun,
their cries shred the silence
of an otherwise perfect morning,
drown out the songs of other birds.

One flies to a branch to criticize
the streets of forever parked cars,
perhaps the tree itself, the wind.

Once, we bred the German Shepherds,
trained them as eyes to lead the blind.
Now our kennels stand silent and empty.
The military took them, maybe even for food.

But the black birds, they are free,
my wife says softly, removing her apron
to help me off with my muddy boots.
Tomorrow I must go find work.
Worry hovers in her eyes.

Sifting the Ashes

I weary of trying to repair what is left,
this roof should last another winter.
She'll manage like she always has,
try to please me, make me laugh.

Too many wars, too many sides
that came and went as we bowed our heads
to passing troops in unfamiliar uniforms,
our own lost long ago.

We are tenants on our own lands
subjected to a tyranny of disharmonic noise
with only those birds to count the days.

She calls them crows.
I call them dog birds.

Price of Freedom

(a door chimes / imaginary conversation)

All we ask is to hear your sad story,
though it's been told countless times.
Welcome, by the way, to the free store.
Feel free to look, take what you need.

We just need to know you're one of *them*.
Wait, no need to share with us, actually,
we can see it in your eyes, your fatigue,
the way you consider that toothpaste.

There's no hint of greed in your hands.
Thoroughly you inspect then move on;
others, those with homes, they take hastily,
while you contemplate each 'purchase.'

Where you're staying, is there much room?
No need to answer that, not our concern.
Lots of shoes and socks to choose from,
yet you decide to walk right past them.

The two of you, you're married?
How much time did you have?
Were you given an evacuation?
We heard most made it out, not—

In the plastic bag is a broken bar of soap,
a single stick of deodorant, a hairbrush,
some dented cans of condensed soup,
enough left behind for others of your kind.

(another chime / nervously a woman leaves)

Out of all the shelves of nonperishables,
you collect what seems like mere rations.
Aren't you hungrier than that, or starved?
Sure you don't want more? Don't answer.

There are toys, too, for your children,
if you have any, clothes for kids as well,
there, opposite side of the warehouse.
Take whatever you need, not to worry.

Probably feels like stealing, doesn't it?
We were only concerned earlier about . . .
well, because the other night some looters,
they brought with them a moving truck.

Smashed through the front windows,
stole the donated mattresses, a dozen,
and other large items meant for you,
such as used furniture and whatnot.

The security cameras captured it all, 1:31 A.M.
No, not victims, and not the regular homeless,
just looters looking to make a quick buck.
Selling everything online or at flea markets.

If you really want to tell your story,
that's okay, but not a requirement.
So . . . please, take more, we insist.
At least fill that plastic Target bag.

What's it like starting completely over?
We didn't—from nothing, we mean—
can't imagine all you've been through,
you and the rest of your family, your—

(another chime as the store empties / a
conversation)

"Why'd they not take much?"
"Who, that couple?"
"Yeah, did they seem picky?"
"Picky?"
"Selective, I mean. When you have nothing—"
"You want nothing."

Looters and Losers

What you see is a line of cars and trucks going out,
What you won't see after are the spoilers slinking in,
most wearing hoodies and sunglasses, faces obscured.

Fucking vultures don't even use protection, but
later, there's the poor guy in line to get his hazmat stuff
before he's allowed to search remains of his property
only to find they beat him to it; his wife's pearls from
the wall safe, his lucky tie clasp and a ruby ring.

Latest you hear, they even got to the donation boxes,
the ones with clothes and food the bastards didn't
     need.
You can bet they posed for selfies with their haul.

Sam T and Krista have a thing going on—
he's got a Ford truck and she loves the thrill
when they're out on the county back roads
trolling for treasure in partly burned homes.
A washer and dryer, a flat screen TV,
not bad for a Thursday, they'll try it again,
the new curfew means nothing to them.

Disposable Hazmat

The mask:
3M N-95,
specifically,
strapped tight,
causing new wrinkles,
and a face covered
in hot-wet breath
within seconds,
a particulate respirator
designed to filter out
what slips between fingers,
and floats in the air,
or disturbed by boot.

The suit:
DuPont Tyvek 400,
specifically,
a disposable
protective cover-all,
sheath of sweat,
baggy beyond control,
not-so "fully breathable,"
as the package states,

with elastic cuffs,
an attached hood,
maybe better suited
for a cleanroom.

The goggles:
Some cheap thing,
specifically,
a plastic gift,
from the government,
came with the gloves,
the booties,
and a lone bottle
of Nestle water
raped from a spring,
and meant to protect
eyes from the airborne,
yet mind the gaps.

The gloves:
Curad Disposable,
specifically,
sterile white,
like everything touched,
powder-free latex
texturized grip,
elastic until torn,
one size too small,
so wear two,
in case objects
slice the skin apart,
letting in contaminants.

The booties:
CleanPro Polyethylene,
specifically,
fits to size 12,
worn over boots
or whatever shoes
have hefty soles,
material thin as tissue,
tough as the suit,
torn open
by a single nail
or ceramic shard,
unable to protect
the space between.

The bag:
Hefty Strong,
specifically,
30-gallon,
1.05 millimeter thick,
multipurpose,
but not today,
blood-red drawstring
at the top,
black as the dead,
meant to hold
all that's worn
post-sift.

At the Clinic

"Stop it, Dr. Vance! Haven't you poked and prodded me enough? I feel fine, just fine. Young man, I'm old enough to be your mother! A woman of my age should be treated with dignity. Nurse, come here with my underthings. What's that? You keep asking if I remember some big fire. I told you, there was no fire! As for finding me wandering outside near the Home? Fiddle-faddle! Yes, I know I'm bandaged. That was your idea. You don't fool me. It's just a ploy to make me get a check-up."

Sands of Time

thrusts his fists into the earth, this man
through white sand as fine as flour
despite a facemask, he tastes
resentment this hour
toxicities, wastes
but all he finds:
black metal
mug-bits
nails

. . .

..

.

..

. . .

rings
dad's coin
mom's silver:
the lost keepsakes
keep turning, he must
until his hands befit cold
the glass dissolved to stardust
a child's handprint fixed in a mold
with luck he'll find mementos, relics

· ·

what he used to have's obliterated
twenty-five hundred fahrenheit
sun-scorched crematorium
a hollowed-out gravesite
death's emporium
toxic remains:
foundation
chimney
rock
· · ·
··
·

Dear Deer

Dear deer,

It was nearly midnight when our high beams found you. The food in the bowl you sniffed is meant for our pet. The other dish, too. Don't worry, that's spring water pulled from some other land not charred, from a bottle. It's safe, and yours if you want it.

We haven't seen signs of life until seeing you. Seems like you're up to your same routine, same path you and your little ones used to follow across our yard. The one we were looking for, when we saw you, used to make strange chirping sounds at you and your family from the window, from inside the house that used to stand, now marked by the chimney headstone. He was always intrigued by your kind. We sat on the porch one afternoon, watched you walk by, a mere ten or so feet away. We stayed quiet, not to disturb you. You saw us, then, didn't seem to mind.

You probably didn't recognize us the other night, since we were in that shiny metal beast whose blinding eyes caused you to startle. Deer in the headlights, that's the old joke. Not so funny now. No offense. Now it makes us cry, knowing you made it out alive. How? We come back each night searching for reflective eyes in the dark, and happened upon yours. It was so good seeing you! Have you seen him, the chirper? You can have some of what we leave out for him each night. Please, we insist.

What little water runs in the creek is unsafe, full of so many chemicals from the unnatural things: plastics, paints, television sets, automobiles . . . well, a number of things that don't concern you, but are also gone. None of that stuff really matters. No living thing needs such things.

Anyway, if you see him out there, the cat, let him know we return each night, looking for his eyes. Sometimes we use the same flashlights we used that horrible night to stumble our way out of the house, since power was out. We found you, which has given us hope that he's still out there, still up to his same routines.

You might think this film on top of everything is snow. Melts off just the same, or would, if rain ever finds us. Wouldn't that be nice? It would as least help end this bad thing. After all this time, nearly a month, it's still not out. This sprinkling each night, it's called ash, the reason we keep coming back. We set out new food, new water, and call his name, but he's never here, most likely forever-gone. But you can have some of the food, if you can stomach it, or, just have the water. If you come back this time tomorrow, what's in the bowls will be fresh. Just save some of each, in case he returns. No need to be greedy.

It was great seeing you again, really, after all this time. And we hope to see you tomorrow as well, and the next . . .

Sincerely,

Your fellow displaced

Vision in a Block of Ice

In the uncertain mist
a woman in a doorway
nurses her child and leers at me.
The edges of her hair glisten.
Escher patterned crystals dance
in her spectral eyes.

Crows on the wire,
a necklace of black stones.
I wonder if she fears the cold,
wonder if she feels it.

The Word

Four simple letters
Uttered / screamed aloud
Could mean almost anything
Kill them . . . *(why did you massacre them?)*

Four characters strung together
Until / perhaps overused
Could be any sort of word
Kill us . . . *(you almost murdered us!)*

Four profound letters
Under- / overused
Could describe every feeling
Kill me . . . *(why didn't you eliminate me?)*

Four characters split apart
Unless / forever adhered
Could explain its power
Kill nothing . . . *(you destroyed nothing!)*

Last Concert

His rival says the f-word
at the Grammys,
gets short-listed for the Nobel
for managing his charities.

"What's it to you," I say.
"You've fans enough waiting
if the fires haven't spread."
But we know they have,
he pretends he doesn't care.

We take the blue bus west.
witch weed blowing in the wind,
the pyramids of downtown Phoenix,
sandstorms and dusky skies.

Hiho and Jojo are twins
named my breasts.
He touches them with his eyes,
plays with my zipper while I sleep.
In Denver we find a hotel
with a ceiling mirror
framed in zircons.

I wait for him to finish,
thinking of a song.

Leftover muffins
on a silver tray,
crumpled napkins.
We drive along the beach.
A Vincent ocean,
thick with ash,
smoke stings our noses,
Los Angeles on fire.

We pass it on the way to
Santa Barbara's Arlington,
where the crowd is packed in tight.
His agent used to bill all concerts
as his last, but this time it's true.

A pretty girl chains herself to stage rail.
She drove clear from Idaho for this.
Maybe she'll get to sleep with him after,
he knows he can, knows I won't care.

Tonight his music bleeds, weaves notes become
a wreath of thorns, make me want to cry.
If it were real, he'd wear it like a Savior
but there's no one left to save, except
perhaps, that kid from Idaho.

Twins Unborn on 9/11

Red dragons scream through hot breath,
rushing in to those running out.
Countless miniature hands cover mouths
so as not to aspirate their fiery breaths
billowing from all directions.
        (gray cauliflower)
        (warm yeast blooms)
An island of multi-millions looks skyward,
changed to identical skin, within seconds,
camouflaged by debris
against a backdrop of terror.

      / a moment earlier:

The first twin inhales,
releases a terrible cough
as the sibling watches in anticipation.

      / a moment later:

The second twin copies his brother,
holds the air a millisecond longer
as if by dare before gasping.

/ now:

A cityscape shrinks in the morning sun,
red dragons swallowed one-by-one.
Monochrome miniature heads glance back
so as not to miss the acrobats
tumbling from all directions.
          (spiraling cartwheels)
          (somersaults)
A once divided class looks downward,
gathers hand-in-hand, within seconds,
amidst shared daydreams of hope
over doubts of survival.

          / a moment earlier:

The first twin falls to his knees,
no longer capable of [under]standing
as the sibling watches in anticipation.

          / a moment later:

The second twin copies his brother,
follows him to the [under]ground
as if lead by example.

          / now:

Not Fair

George stands speechless watching the scene unfold.
There's the plane bee-lining into one World Trade
    tower,
a heartbeat, smoke, and soon enough the crumpling
    horror—
then the second plane on course into the twin,
smoke overwhelms the sky, a black and deadly snow
    begins.
Invasion, soon the bombs would come, we'll all die
    today!
After the searing fear, he's angry. He's a newlywed,
only twenty-seven, with a lifetime still ahead, unfair!

But no bombs come, the cities of America live on.
The footage continues to be news for weeks,
FDNY are there for days digging through ash for
    victims,
knowing the risk would mark them casualties as well.

Eighteen years later, George watches a former talk
    show host
stand in front of Congress with a dying former
    fireman,

pleading for continued compensation for the first
    responders.
There is a new President, a new regime with other
    priorities,
like golden faucets in the White House bathroom.
But say, such attacks are buried in the past,
precautions are in place, another 9/11 can't happen
    again.
That's dangerous thinking, and not a thing about it's
    fair.

Cartwheels

They fly like superheroes
Arms outstretched
Scarves flapping as capes
Swan dives
Pencil dives
Cannonballs
Hands holding hands
So as not to be alone
In the empty sky
Clouds float like battleships
Over an ocean of asphalt

They fly like superheroes
Hand-over-hand
Feet-over-feet
Tiny silhouettes
Five-pointed stars
Falling through daylight
Pinwheels
Tumbleweeds
Acrobats
The world flips
Down becomes up

In Media Res

Fires:
misreported,
caught on film from afar,
mammoth clouds of smoke; damage yet
unknown.

Classroom
children asking
what happened to their friends,
teacher gives up trying to teach
today

Viewers
unblinkingly
stare at televisions
unsure how to react, or help,
useless.

Panic
dies down slowly;
victims find the shelters,
their worldly goods forever gone
by dawn.

Patient
hugs corgi close;
nurse treats them both for burns,
makes room for the pair in the ward
tonight.

Burnt homes,
outlines, really,
smolder for days untouched,
mass-counted by drone flyovers,
leveled.

Sobbing,
a little girl
clutches her baby doll;
fires have claimed its face, there's not much
to hold.

Displaced,
far too many,
seek shelter where they can;
thousands instantly turned homeless
worry.

Anchors,
cameras live,
unsure what to report,
relay estimated numbers—
guesses.

Michael Bailey and Marge Simon

Choppers
fly overhead;
aerial shots of black,
perimeter lines of orange
growing.

Coverage

Insurance should cover it all
if every payment's made
in full,
on time.

Miss or undercut by a cent
and they will hang you
out to dry,
the lot of you.

Hundreds of thousands
in interior damage
for things,
just stuff.

Designed to replenish
if nothing remains
of anything,
except rubble.

How much coverage shall be paid
to replace without question
one's pet,
a life?

What if assurances are denied
because one's location
is at risk,
amid trees?

Take these extra dollars
before payment is due
to help me,
not you.

Symptoms

D is for discerning soot in the nose,
>   A bad sore throat will add to your woes.
E is for eyes, a watery-red,
>   Rinse with salt water, then off to bed.
A is for abdomen's stabbing pain,
>   Things can get worse, the fires are to blame.
T is for traces of blood in the cough
>   Get away from smoke, you've had enough.
H is for headache that won't go away.
>   With plenty of rest, you should be okay.

Masked

An entire population of surgeons amasses, of nurses,
of those afraid to breathe. But it's not Halloween. No
one's in costume.

Particulates, the new catchphrase, along with *air-
quality-index, aspirated, just stuff, cancer*, both *the
missing* and *the dead*.

An entire population knows them by name, N-95, for
they are backordered online, sold-out in-store,
bought high demand. 3M.

Those who need them are unable because those-who-
don't buy in surplus, wanting to help, but deplete
necessities instead.

An entire population breathes what-used-to-be *stuff*,
the missing and *the dead*, hands to unfiltered noses
and mouths.

By the time the order arrives, months too late,
cancer's spread to lungs, across state, country,
creating new mock-medical staff.

The Unforgiving Tree

Once there were two trees and two little boys. One of the trees was an apple tree, the other a Ponderosa pine. Both little boys loved trees. The apple tree was a Giving Tree, and wound up being used over and over until finally she was just a stump for her (once little) boy to sit on. The pine wasn't so friendly. When the other little boy tried to climb it, he quickly returned to the ground with scratched legs and ant bites. But he was a boy, he said he didn't mind. He grew up, had a family of three, his house made of the pine's kindred. He decided the pine would be their first Christmas tree.

> winter comes again,
> we give you all we have
> still you ask for more

Yet the pine grew tallest of her sisters. She wasn't sorry to be too tall for the coming occasion. Bitterly she'd watched for years as her (once little) boy and his kind kept robbing the forest. They gave nothing in return, not even a *thank-you-kindly*. It was the same as what happened to the loving apple tree. This was not right. Come years of drought, the trees were dry and thirsty.

When fires erupted due to human error, the Ponderosa's pathway to justice was clear. She joined the conflagration, urging her sisters to follow.

> we choose flames
> to bring renewal
> deserve us

Take My Forest

Take my lawn, so long as you need:
    setup a tent, the sprinklers are off for the draught
    bring your infant child, we'll warm some milk
    here's a blanket or two, keep yourselves warm
    don't mind the noise, just neighborhood
        generators
    shouldn't drop below the 40s, but bundle up tight
    in the morning we'll make cocoa, talk long-term . . .

Take my trailer, so long as you need:
    hitch it to the back of your truck, out of the smoke
    business parking lots, they're letting people stay
    next to the river, a few campsites if you hurry
    what about friends, do they have a spare side
        yard?
    food cooked on sticks over pit-fire, sounds nice
    family campout the next few days, perhaps
        months . . .

Take my room, so long as you need:
    our child can manage without, can bunk with
        siblings
    you sure the four of you are fine, cozy in there?

don't mind the mess, and no it's not a problem
the house might be chaotic, lots of visitors recently
park wherever you can, around other guests
hope there's room in recycling, for empty bottles . . .

Take my house, so long as you need:
    bring all your belongings, doesn't seem like much
    the place is furnished, use the dressers and beds
    don't worry about rent, we'll figure it out later
    there's enough room to stretch, not so cramped
    and the kids can play outside, the air clear
    call this place "home," at least until spring . . .

Take my forest, so long as you need:
    the trees are used to this ruin, ever-thirsty
    hasn't rained for most of the year, hopefully soon
    winds will snap limbs, downing powerlines
    may want to grab a few things, whatever you can
    most of this land will be made barren, overnight
    a human cleanse, so nature can breathe again . . .

Beneath the Cold of Cities, Dark

Before ice claimed the world above,
we slept on cardboard mattresses
with rags for pillows, cozied up or lying
on hot air vents to stay alive in winter
& survived on someone's leftovers.

Beneath the cities
we homeless endured,
for we were the experts.

Spread your legs for a poke,
or offer your ass, cash only
to get what you need

that's how it used to be for some,
for others, begs in your casket
for a bottle of forget

not so now, nothing outside for pay
nothing inside for your habits
so you adapt, you barter

Old Marie lights the candles,
& another mural begins on a new wall,
a sort of Lascaux thing.

Longman T claps his hands to set the beat.

Of life and alive, the wall mirrors forms & faces,
eyes / hands / mouths / souls, a perfect synergy
in an underground world with no boundaries.

We've got sewers
We have rats
Food & water
We tell ourselves
We'll survive.

Wor(O)ds Dissolve

With a length of aluminum
Melted tire rim
Re-solidified
You prod a block
Flash-fired
Thousands of degrees
Books alongside books
Once trapped in a box
Unsold novels, collections
Wherein seemingly nothing's written
The metal pushes through
Softly separates the mass
One side falls away, crumbles
Type still there
Sentences
Paragraphs
Characters
Imaginary people
Autobiographical plot
You are a god
And you read the words
Recognize passages
"I wrote that," you say

"I gave that story life"
"I created—"
The words dissolve
As you touch them, gloved
Pages turn to powder
Worlds ruined
Stardust
The mind snaps
Delicate, like hard candy
You toss everything away
Put your boot through the past

Survivalism

Every meal could be the last, and so why not eat like a prisoner, arms out at angles, protectively, around the plate or whatever?
Survival-eating.

The goal is to cram it down in as little time as possible: seconds, minutes, or longer. Food is food. Enjoyment no longer matters. What matters is to do what's necessary to continue waking up in the morning. Protein intake, carbohydrates, vitamins, the essentials. Make a pill to swallow; that's the future of nutrition.

Funny how water has no taste, yet everyone keeps drinking, and those who complain about its tastelessness are always putting something into it, but for what purpose? It takes more energy to enjoy something than to not, so why give it any effort?

Primitive mastication, quickly learned. Hot food or cold, doesn't matter much. Room-temp water. Ice? What for? Seldom are there left-overs, because it all goes down the human garbage disposal instead saved for later discarding.

The first few days after the fire left little time to enjoy one's diet. The learning part's easy. Endless coffee for burnout energy, and once hitting rock-bottom, more to feed the addiction.

Sometimes alcohol to attempt the impossibilities of sleep, because that's also required. Got a few hours the first week of the fires, the lack of which makes you wonder about reality and about its opposite, and what's really important.

I catch myself at the end of a meal, or a nap, both at once sometimes, staring at an empty plate, wondering what happened to it all, if anyone minded my mind-absence. Not surprising how similar eating has become to sleep-less-walking, those little slips into unconsciousness while awake, or while driving.

Around other people, I base my eating habits on theirs so as not to appear too animalistic, although I am in fact an animal, more so now than ever before. A wolf, wolfing. A malnutritioned animal, maybe. Chew, I tell myself. Enjoy. Did I get any on me? Sometimes. Slow down, I tell myself. Try to at least act normal.

Why? Because it's expected of you. Here, put some flavor in your water. Eat slower. Taste what you're putting in there. But still, I scarf every potential last-meal. Who knows? Could be.

And now I understand why the cat eats and drinks the way he does, having survived running from a fire for twenty-three days straight. Nothing to eat but charred, flavorless death; nothing to ingest but toxic-flavored water. The stuff in the tap, how bad is it now that everything's settled? Every sip, perhaps the last.

The Final Season

Winter wears long hands,
miles of white on the horizon.

Mama boiled their dog,
but Ringo was already very thin,
so his meat was tough and spare.
Their baby brother, Thomas,
was born after things got bad.

He is too weak to eat, doesn't
cry, his diaper goes unused.
There are three children to feed,
Their mother has no choice.

Stationed in no-man's-land,
our outpost meant to be a haven
for civilian survivors, we once had
food and medicines, but no more.

We've become stick-men in uniform,
sunken faced and hollow eyed;
hunger clawing at our guts
like a cat trapped in a bag.

Kreuger falls, won't get up, won't talk.
He's been sick for days,
frostbite has claimed his feet,
already he smells like a dead thing.

As we stand around him,
Hudson begins tapping his bowl
against his rifle, licks his lips.
I make us wait; it won't be long now
before he draws his last breath.

Once there was a time of seasons,
turn again, there's only one.

Forever Hungry Drums

Homeless strike up their war drums,
tossing in any and all flammables
they can find not worth hoarding.

'Fifty-five gallon' stamped upon
once satiated stomachs, emptied,
purged of liquid waste, up-ended.

Uncovered, the roaring instruments
are forever unfulfilled, always fed,
open mouths spitting cursed heat.

All which burns gets tossed inside
as an endless growing army gathers
to stay warm, uniformed in stench.

Behind make-shift tarps and tents
they prop up cardboard barricades,
behind stolen grocery cart tanks.

At night these soldiers pilfer through
refuse bins in search of recyclables,
garbage transformed to cash for fuel.

Tired lives walk the battle forefront
in stained holey-ripped cast-asides,
thrift-sifted forgotten non-goodwill.

Each night a new battle commences
over food, water, shelter, basic need;
the weathered and wounded told:

Defecate elsewhere, off the streets,
a disgrace of humankind, of decency,
take this mess away from here, leave!

Police and fire are called to serve:
to relocate, to use force if required;
transfer, arrest, whatever it takes . . .

Forever-hungry drums are silenced,
but not for very long, for the horde
drifts, mimicking bird murmuration.

Left behind is a wake of trash, needles,
street-swept into the past, forgotten,
remnants of a ceaseless non-problem.

Fifty-five gallons, all ash evacuated,
strike gonglike when tipped aside,
snare-rattle if rolled along sidewalk.

Thousands march in soundless stride,
a woeful parade of forced relocation,
for there's no place to live outdoors.

Nectar of the Gods

How long does it take for a man to drink himself to
    death?
Not of our fine Cabernet, nor any other from our
    vineyards,
No, he waters his besotted mind with whiskey, any
    kind.

His disposition started long before the fires, but in his
    broken state
he thought the industry was doomed, for he could see
    the flames
and smell the burning of a thousand vines. It was his
    Armageddon.

Only a year ago, he was so sure the tours would end,
    with no green
life to view, nor wines enough for tastings, we'd need
    to raise the costs
of keg and case, best likely year for reds now swallowed
    by the fires.

Yet visitors returned twofold, exceeding prior years,
    our coffers filled.
Vineyards even served as firebreaks, limiting the
    spread of passage.
Insurance paid for damage, our budding vines
    resumed, but not for him.

We leave him be, the fool must have his way.

Startled Awake

The smallest noise
opens his eyes.

He cannot sleep
for fear of waking.

What is that siren
in the distance?

The soft patter
of helicopter beats.

His own heart
pounds unsteadily similar.

Each blown-out candle
reminds him of the wind.

Bursting birthday balloons
like car explosions.

What is that silence
in the other room?

Please be the child
falling into dream.

Victims Three

At first you need comfort, to be held tightly,
To be told you're going to be all right.
Some will need it for years to come,
Others won't want to be touched at all.

Colin thinks he can still feel
the bloody scratches from his cat
he didn't hold tight enough
the night of the firestorm,
but that was months ago.

Kid dreams the same awful dream—
over and over, hearing Lily
yowling up ahead, but the trees are
all on fire, and though he tries so hard,
she's always just beyond his reach.

Sara was to be crowned
Homecoming Queen next Saturday,
but there will be no celebration—
no expensive gown (now ash),
or pricey dyed-to-match heels (charred),
no requisite corsage of roses.

She doesn't care about any of it now.
Safe in a refuge
from the burning hills,
she starts writing a letter
to her boyfriend,
writing and writing
until the pen runs dry, but she
doesn't stop, can't stop
pressing the pen to the page—
I love you I love you I love you,
until her hand cramps, and
she can't stop shaking.

Rob is a 'Nam Vet,
has serious trauma issues.
Doc gave him a prescription
to relieve the nightmares,
he's deep asleep when the first
embers land in his front yard.
Smoke enfolds him in its deadly blanket.
Too late, he tries to wake up.

He won't be needing pills to sleep,
won't have the memory of a little girl
holding her momma's hand
just before she's blown in half.
or the look in a gook's eyes when
Rob bayonets him in the gut.
Maybe Rob's a lucky guy after all;
one horrendous waking nightmare
is enough for any life.

Let Me Go, Please

I don't want your embrace,
so let me go,
give me space.

I don't need conversation,
so close that mouth,
heed the dissuasion.

I don't care to hear your story,
so don't ask me mine,
the mind's a quarry.

I don't require empathy
so please just listen,
not all need sympathy.

I don't have your attention,
so wipe those tears,
understand my condition.

I don't feel like talking,
so be on your way,
persistence is stalking.

I don't accept your tenacity,
so take a step back,
post-trauma veracity.

Fire Sale

1. 1920 Underwood Portable typewriter, slight damage to carriage, etc.

2. Child's hand imprint plaque circa 2014, turquoise enamel

3. Terracotta chunk with child's initials, circa 2007

4. Steel handlebars for a ten-speed bicycle, will clean up nicely

5. Two boxes flat-head nails, mixed sizes, slightly discolored

6. Slate sign "LESS OUR HOME", missing the "B"

There Until Remembered

You are an amputee:
both arms attached,
ten fingers intact;
feeling for nothing,
itching the past.

(where did it go?)

You reach inside the closet
for the rayon red blouse,
the one with yellow daisies,
grabbing instead a pullover
provided by a friend.
It's the least favorite
but will suffice.

You reach for the ladle
mixed in with the spatulas,
solid stainless-steel,
rummaging in drawers.
No, not there either,
perhaps in the dishwasher,
a measuring cup will do.

(feasibly misplaced it)

You call out in the night
for the golden retriever
always next to the bed,
snoring so soundly.
The weight at your feet
only the throw blanket
to keep you warm.

You call him on the phone,
let it ring seven times,
eventually hearing his voice,
and it makes you sob.
No message this time,
the mailbox full;
button pressed to redial.

(where could he have—?)

You expect to find joy
in your child's laughter,
but even that's destroyed,
a broken doll.
The smiles turn flat,
split foundation;
all that remains.

You expect to have closure,
not realizing what's gone,
erased from normalcy.
Forgotten until remembered,

these ghost relics
haunt everyday life,
only there in the mind.

(must be somewhere)

You are an amputee:
both legs present,
ten toes numb;
standing for something,
walking on memory.

Who Are You?

You don't have a driver's license,
not even a wallet?
You don't have a passport,
or identification of any kind?
You don't have your registration,
nor a laminated photograph?

Who are you?

You don't have insurance paperwork,
not even a utility bill?
You don't have your green card,
or a visa of any kind?
You don't have a paystub,
nor a previous tax return?

Who are you?

You don't have a cell phone,
not even a tablet?
You don't have a laptop,
or a computer of any kind?
You don't have internet access,
nor a way to communicate?

Who are you?

You don't have a home,
not even a bed?
You don't have cash or credit,
or money of any kind?
You don't have means to buy food,
nor clean water?

Who are you?

You don't have evidence of self,
not even a living relative?
You don't have an identity,
or paperwork of any kind?
You don't have a way to prove existence,
nor confirmation of past?

Who are you?

You don't have anything,
not even a life?
You don't have verification,
or documentation on hand?
You don't have any of those,
nor a way to obtain them again?

Who are you?

Fresh Canvas

A boy of about ten
stands in the middle of a plot
where all is ash and rubble.
His face is dirty, tear-stained.
He watches as an old man in a straw hat
selects a spot and sets up an easel.

"You wondering why I'm here, boy?"
The boy nods, "Yeah, Mister.
My family, we used to live here
couple years ago, but the fires—
why are you painting this?
It's ugly, I hate it!"

The old man smiles,
prepares his palette.
"Pretend you're an artist.
What you see is a painting
you thought was finished,
but something happened,
something changed,
& the life-color is gone,
like what's before us.

Watch what I'm doing,
see how you can fix it.
Starting with a cobalt wash,
layer in your viridian, like so,
add a tinge of Prussian blue
& daubs of yellow ochre,
a bit of Cad yellow,
I mix again, apply—
see what I'm up to?

Grass, flowers, saplings—
make it happen with the brush,
in time, you'll have a home again,
a yesterday memory, modified,
with new walls, a roof—
within a year the rest,
if you are willing.

It'll be *different,*
kind of like an altered canvas,
& underneath the new, remains
the phantom of the old—
you follow me young fella?"

The boy looks at the ruins, then
back to the fresh painting.
Slowly he begins to smile.
"My dad, mister,
he needs to see this."

One Vacant Lot

The neighborhood rebuilds,
lots filled, dead trees uprooted;
a few hundred homes raised
before the anniversary,
praised by the poised media
noise-polluted with construction,
and can it work for me?
each ask themselves,
watching skeleton frames rise,
twice in size, pointed rafters
piercing the skies,
builders high on greed
as they feed a need for excess
not suited for lower- or any-class,
perhaps a thousand or more homes
shoved up the county's ass
by year two,
us too!
and who knew by three
this number would double;
debt-free, no . . .
no, there's trouble
while some flee out-of-state

once-owners-turned-moaners,
forced into upgrades,
higher rates,
blueprints slid under noses,
sad fates, full plates,
initial here, and here, and here . . .
decisions made over phone,
behind closed doors,
choosing floors,
and don't ignore exterior,
fingers pointing,
anointing the land,
drought-resistant plants,
slats of slate,
rocks as groundcover,
gravel-yards flocked with pots,
no need to water the lawn, only the roof,
walls made fire-retardant;
single-shingled roofs,
solar tiles for miles,
asphalt, stone-coated steel,
all this expense, will it save?
though it doesn't seem real,
and won't matter with heat;
as the mind reels,
tough decisions,
these rough-precision designs,
funds frozen, resigned
while commuting in Escalades;
money fades, fades, fades . . .
owners coerced to sign
on the dotted line,
cost of supplies jacked

over dreamless slumber,
inflated imported lumber,
minds racked, hacked,
lost in thought,
before it all,
before the flames found . . .
before the wind . . .
before, before, before the bubble
when will it pop?
gets slit by the bank,
and who to thank?
debt-to-income ratio sank,
now standard,
these vaulted ceilings,
anxious feelings,
untraditional rooms,
halted plans,
no more children,
to compensate as price inflates,
maybe try when it's over . . .
and so there's a need,
not greed, for granite counters,
hardwood floors, upgraded doors,
as cash is counted,
recounted, unaccounted;
no chimneys this time around,
the money handed out,
no doubt
by the tens-and hundreds-of-thousands,
piled in mounds;
three- and four-car garages built
without reason or guilt,
to hold all this stuff,

filled, filled, filled . . .
and as the years pass,
unwatered artificial turf,
sacrificial, these yards,
to save resources,
not in the cards;
another year gone,
nearly all homes rebuilt,
and yet a lone lot,
among the rest
one spot,
untouched;
who owns that land?
and someone ought—
no, no one sought
to find her . . .
why not?

The Poem at the End of the World

Composing his last poem, the poet walks the beach at the end of the world. His lover lags behind, a bag over her shoulder. The ocean is heavy with death. He pauses, waits for his lover to catch up. She takes her time, picking up the prettiest shells which she places in the bag. She is bent nearly double with the burden, but it is her choice to follow him.

Just after sunset, the poet and his lover come upon a cage. There is a strange wingless bird locked within. Hunkering down, the poet inscribes his words in the sand beneath the cage. His lover covers them with the contents of her bag.

The poet takes her hand. "We've done all we can. My poem, your shells, are the business of the sea. They are no longer yours or mine. Perhaps they never were." This is all there is to be said. Together they unlock the cage, but the bird remains inside. They lie down on the beach, holding each other close throughout the night.

Sunrise comes. They wake to see the ocean is again alive, and the bird has grown wings. It rises on the wind and disappears into a perfect blue which is neither sky nor dream.

Paper Earth

We make our way to the writing ground,
paper-white, as far as any eye can see,
where exhausted trees no longer shed.

What time is it, but does that matter,
and can life be measured such a way?

Rain will soon seal everything together,
forlorn-fallen tears cementing in layers,
where blackened trunks stand as sentinels.

What to write, fill the thoughts of few,
as each word cuts deep, *every last thing.*

We wait patiently for the clouds to part,
expecting the hands of angry gods,
yet humankind's fingers do the pointing.

Sifting the Ashes

Who's fault is this, and should we care,
one way or the other, *and is it too late?*

Countless stories are carved in the earth,
until every last broken finger is bled,
not-so-forever tales of what once was.

We were here, some layers will read,
existence recorded semi-permanently.

But well before the expected rainfall,
Father's clock of life will tilt, tilt, tilt,
as Mother lets out her sighing breath.

You were never here, She will whisper,
and His hourglass will flip, *begin again.*

Counting the Offering

It's after Sunday worship,
Ms. Ellie in the backroom
counts the offering;
just one plate needed,
only two rows of folks
to occupy the pews.

The church is very old,
made of timber, unscathed
by fires throughout decades.
Pastor Ross didn't show this time,
some say he lost his home.

She knows the truth,
knows he's just tired of it,
maybe even lost his faith,
but she's okay with that.
Sad, but he's got a right.

Justin T. led the service,
giving thanks for being spared,
His big voice deep and steady,
his message ringing true:

Sifting the Ashes

More hazards yet to come—
things like these fires,
the Lord isn't testing us,
we'll be testing one another.

The dollar bills, she smooths out
carefully together in her hand,
proud that she's entrusted,
plenty of time for a task she loves.

A Return to Normalcy

Now that it's over, with these scars,
the planet's hesitation marks, perhaps,
a return to normalcy for all . . .

No, one tragedy replaces the next,
coverage only concerned about the now,
#breaking_news, #new_normal.

The burn of concern turns viral,
humankind erupting from within,
a fever-fire; don't panic, not yet . . .

Once again come the white masks,
but not for smoke inhalation concern,
as the horde hoards what's vital.
Curfews and closings, it only gets worse,
all sports officially off the scene,
nothing to watch but reruns and news.

Schools shut down, no entry allowed, but
who'll feed a low-income family's child
when their daily hot meal is no more?

Homebirth your babies, hospitals are filled.
For a year, all weddings postponed;
no travel abroad, you're stuck where you are.

Stock market plunges, recession looms,
when will your paycheck arrive?
Washing your hands doesn't pay the bills.

There are some who say it's no big deal,
they're feeling fine, but there's no nightlife,
with the bars and eateries closed.

Parents transform dining tables to offices,
the kids each in their (class)rooms, bored,
screens burning assignments into tired minds.

Shelter-in-place orders demanded by the State,
half the nation closed, mandatory seclusion;
misdemeanors issued if caught outdoors.

Will they arrest you for buying baby formula
on the black market, or for milk to freeze?
Just about every damn grocery isle's bare.

You reach past the elderly, no sign of greed;
she can't get the last bottle: acetaminophen.
Ibuprofen only aggravates the heat, is rumored.

Coughing into your sleeve, you wonder
about the inferno, and exponential growth,
as droplets of sweat dapple your brow.

Yet you're not alone, fixes are at hand.
restaurants offer curbside pick-up,
deliveries from grocery stores, fast food.

Drive-thru lunches for *all* children
coming faster than you'd dreamed,
parks and playgrounds for the home-bound.

A neighborly friend wants to share,
no guns involved, pool resources with them;
you have the produce, they've got fresh milk.

As with virus, fire, or hurricane,
if you can't always get what you want,
be grateful to get what you need.

The end?

**Not if you want to dive into more of Crystal Lake
Publishing's Tales from the Darkest Depths!**

Check out our amazing website and online store.
https://www.crystallakepub.com

We always have great new projects and content on
the website to dive into, as well as a newsletter,
behind the scenes options, social media platforms,
our own dark fiction shared-world series and our
very own webstore. If you use the IGotMyCLPBook!
coupon code in the store (at the checkout), you'll get
a one-time-only 50% discount on your first eBook
purchase!

Our webstore even has categories specifically for KU
books, non-fiction, anthologies, novels, novellas. and
of course poetry collections.

Michael Bailey is a recipient of the Bram Stoker Award, Benjamin Franklin Award, and a Shirley Jackson Award nominee. He has authored numerous novels, standalone novellas and novelettes, fiction and poetry collections, and runs the small press Written Backwards where he edits and publishes anthologies.

Marge Simon was born in Bethesda, MD, but grew up in Boulder, CO.

She received her BA and MA degrees from the University of Northern Colorado, and then continued her studies at the Art Center College of Design. Deciding against a career as a commercial artist, she began working as an art teacher in elementary schools instead.

In the mid-1980s, Simon began writing and illustrating for the small press and went on to become an award-winning writer. Simon's poems, short fiction, and illustrations have appeared in hundreds of publications, including *Amazing Stories*, *Nebula Awards 32*, *Strange Horizons*, *The Pedestal Magazine*, *Chizine*, *Niteblade*, *Vestal Review*, and *Daily Science Fiction*.

Simon is a former president of the Small Press Writers and Artists Organization and of the Science Fiction & Fantasy Poetry Association (SFPA). She is additionally a former editor of Star*Line, the SFPA's bimonthly journal.

In 2013, Simon began editing the column "Blood and Spades: Poets of the Dark Side" for the monthly newsletter of the Horror Writers Association (HWA). She serves as the Chair of the HWA Board of Trustees. Simon lives in Ocala, Florida, with her husband, writer Bruce Boston, with whom she sometimes collaborates.

Poems by Michael Bailey:
Blink
Mon Autumn
Angel Wings of Death
Orange Borealis
Loosed Earth
Diggin' Ghosts
Past the Past
Arcing
Sleep, Child
The Great Build-up
First to Respond
A Warning
Freebird
Life (C)remains
Weapons of Mass Distraction
Who Will Teach Them?
Kilned
The Nocturnal Waking Nightmare
Blocked
The Devil's Matchsticks
23 Days
Arachnid
Sleep, What Might It Bring?
Birthday Deathbed
Wings Outstretched
Night-swimming
Conflagration
Crawling Mountains
Weather, Simplified
The Longest Drive
Spread Thin
Beneath Clouds
What Day Is This?
Moonscape

More Poetry collections by Crystal Lake Publishing:

Readers . . .

Thank you for reading *Sifting the Ashes*. We hope you enjoyed this collection of poetry.

If you have a moment, please review *Sifting the Ashes* at the store where you bought it.

Help other readers by telling them why you enjoyed this book. No need to write an in-depth discussion. Even a single sentence will be greatly appreciated. Reviews go a long way to helping a book sell, and is great for an author's career. It'll also help us to continue publishing quality books. You can also share a photo of yourself holding this book with the hashtag #IGotMyCLPBook!

Thank you again for taking the time to journey with Crystal Lake Publishing.

Visit our Linktree page for a list of our social media platforms. https://linktr.ee/CrystalLakePublishing

the problems so they can stay in a creative mind. Which of course also means paying our authors.

We do not just publish books, we present to you worlds within your world, doors within your mind, from talented authors who sacrifice so much for a moment of your time.

There are some amazing small presses out there, and through collaboration and open forums we will continue to support other presses in the goal of helping authors and showing the world what quality small presses are capable of accomplishing. No one wins when a small press goes down, so we will always be there to support hardworking, legitimate presses and their authors. We don't see Crystal Lake as the best press out there, but we will always strive to be the best, strive to be the most interactive and grateful, and even blessed press around. No matter what happens over time, we will also take our mission very seriously while appreciating where we are and enjoying the journey.

What do we offer our authors that they can't do for themselves through self-publishing?

We are big supporters of self-publishing (especially hybrid publishing), if done with care, patience, and planning. However, not every author has the time or inclination to do market research, advertise, and set up book launch strategies. Although a lot of authors are successful in doing it all, strong small presses will always be there for the authors who just want to do what they do best: write.

What we offer is experience, industry knowledge, contacts and trust built up over years. And due to our strong brand and trusting fanbase, every Crystal Lake Publishing book comes with weight of respect. In time our fans begin to trust our judgment and will try a new author purely based on our support of said author.

With each launch we strive to fine-tune our approach, learn from our mistakes, and increase our reach. We continue to assure our authors that we're here for them and that we'll carry the weight of the launch and dealing with third parties while they focus on their strengths—be it writing, interviews, blogs, signings, etc.

We also offer several mentoring packages to authors that include knowledge and skills they can use in both traditional and self-publishing endeavours.

We look forward to launching many new careers.

This is what we believe in. What we stand for. This will be our legacy.

**Welcome to Crystal Lake Publishing—
Tales from the Darkest Depths.**